The Love Gamble

Other Avalon Books by Lauren M. Phelps

THE UNSETTLED HEART
DANGEROUS RECKONING
AFTER HARVEST COMES

THE
LOVE GAMBLE

LAUREN M. PHELPS

AVALON BOOKS
THOMAS BOUREGY AND COMPANY, INC.
401 LAFAYETTE STREET
NEW YORK, NEW YORK 10003

© Copyright 1993 by Lauren M. Phelps
Library of Congress Catalog Card Number: 92-97232
ISBN 0-8034-8972-2
All rights reserved.
All the characters in this book are fictitious,
and any resemblance to actual persons,
living or dead, is purely coincidental.

PRINTED IN THE UNITED STATES OF AMERICA
ON ACID-FREE PAPER
BY HADDON CRAFTSMEN, SCRANTON, PENNSYLVANIA

To Sue, who believed in me before I believed in myself,
and who never lets me give up, even when I want to.

Chapter One

Ice and snow whirled eerily through a wispy fog, cutting visibility to near zero, as Joanna Christenson headed south out of Princeton, Iowa. She slowed the old station wagon to a crawl and wished she were back in Texas. How could the weather be so bad in mid-November?

She should never have ventured out of her snug LeClaire apartment. She wouldn't have if she'd known what awaited her. But the old man had seemed like such a good lead. And he'd been friendly on the phone, so she had bundled up and driven almost thirty miles to Clinton in the middle of a blizzard.

The old man had seemed pleasant enough when she arrived at Clinton Care 'n' Share, but the plush offices should have clued her in.

1

No respectable charity would waste money on such thick carpet, such fancy furniture. And the door she had passed through had named him the organization's director.

Still, he had looked like a perfectly nice old guy, with his shiny, gray-fringed head and alert blue eyes. Small and wiry, he had grinned as he shook her hand and asked how he could help her.

Once she started talking, his smile had faded, fast.

"My family records? You want to poke around in my family records? You must be kidding!"

"Why, no, sir," she had answered. "I'm writing a book about riverboats on the Mississippi, and I'd heard that you might be able to help me."

She hadn't managed another word. Leaping up from his leather chair, he had paced around the office as he delivered a loud, angry diatribe. Jo couldn't remember all of it, but invasion of privacy, meddling, and nosy women had figured prominently.

Jo had put up with ten minutes of abuse before she'd stood to go. Glaring down at his balding head, she'd said, "A simple 'no' would have been sufficient."

Then she had walked out, slamming the door behind her.

It was hard to believe Joseph Porter was in charge of a charitable organization. Did he shout at the people he was supposed to help too? Jo didn't think she wanted to know.

What concerned her at the moment was her poor book. How was she going to write a fresh, interesting account of riverboat gambling without any new material? Not that her editor was pressing her for miracles—he had been quite pleased to hear that she was actually working on one of the new gambling boats to get the flavor of the river.

The book would come out fine if she had to depend on libraries and historical-society records, but Jo wasn't shooting for "fine." Nothing less than "wonderful" would do, if she had anything to say about it. Which meant she'd better do some more digging. Someone in the Quad-Cities *must* have some old diaries stuck back in his basement or attic.

As she crept along the road, watching for icy spots, snow gave way to rain, but the dirty white fog swirled even thicker. Jo glared at her watch. Not yet noon, yet it could be dusk, it was so dark. She was surprised the rain didn't wash the fog away, but mist rose steadily off the river.

A flash of color on the gravel shoulder caught her eye. Someone was stranded. She pulled over and braked in front of the stalled auto. Slipping her slim shoulders into her threadbare camel coat, she untangled her long, dark-brown hair from the collar and went to investigate.

The car was empty, its emergency lights

blinking. But what a car it was—a Mercedes convertible, new and fiery red. Jo shook her head in astonishment. Who would be dumb enough to leave his car rather than wait for help in this weather? Some people just didn't have any sense. Of course, what could you expect of someone who would spend that kind of money on a car? She climbed back into the wagon without bothering to shed her coat.

With a final glance at the Mercedes, she steered carefully back onto the road. She felt a guilty twinge of satisfaction at its owner's misfortune as she watched the roadside. At least she wasn't the only one having a rotten Monday.

She found the driver a mile or so down the road, plodding through the slushy snow. A soggy fur coat identified him as the Mercedes' owner. More conspicuous consumption. Jo shook her head as she pulled over and rolled down her window. "Isn't it a bit cool for a walk?"

"I guess it is." The man looked confused.

"Can I give you a ride somewhere?"

"Do you always pick up strangers?" He frowned at her but made no move to get in.

Jo bristled with irritation. That was the second time today a stranger had criticized her. And she'd been trying to do a good deed! She almost drove off and left him, but he looked wet and miserable. She couldn't ignore his crack, though. "You don't look like much of a threat. I'd say you're in worse shape than your car," she drawled.

"Oh, you saw the car. I should have real-ized." To her surprise, the man laughed, brushing at the ice clinging to his coat. He had a nice voice, warm and deep. "Sorry if I sounded bossy, but I have a younger sister. It's sort of a habit. Have I lost my chance for a ride?"

She couldn't stop the smile that tickled her lips. "Of course not. Get in before you freeze."

The man slipped into the front seat, pulled off his gloves, and extended a hand. "I really appreciate this. I'm Rob Porter, from Daven-port."

Porter. Now there was a familiar name, though this friendly stranger was nothing like the Porter she'd just tangled with. Hadn't she read somewhere that people with the same names tended to be alike? Obviously it wasn't true. Or maybe that only applied to first names or to relatives.

Rob clearly wasn't related to grumpy old Joseph Porter. Besides being nearly twice the old man's size, he was too nice, and Porter was a common name. There must be twenty Porters in Davenport alone, and the old man lived in Clinton. She guessed she shouldn't blame Rob for having the same name.

His icy hand closed over her slim fingers in a firm handshake. Her hand seemed to disappear in his. "Joanna Christenson, Jo to my friends. Glad to meet you."

She turned the heater up before easing the car into gear. That gave her a moment to study her passenger. He was nice looking, with thick, wavy black hair worn a little long, and expressive brown eyes. Though the lines of his face were too strong to be conventionally handsome, he was still strikingly attractive. And he was big. His broad shoulders filled the front seat. But why notice that? She was just giving him a ride. "You should dry out pretty quick with the heater on. What's wrong with your car?"

"Who knows? I'd just pulled onto the highway when it coughed a couple of times and died. That car is only three months old. It should work." Rob grimaced.

Jo pressed her lips together to hide a smile. "You did check the gas gauge, didn't you?"

"Of course I...." He paused, blinking. "I'm not sure. I was a bit upset when I left Frances's house." He pulled a jeweler's box out of his pocket and flipped it open. A huge diamond solitaire rested on the black velvet. "This little beauty is to blame." A rueful grin softened his face, making him even more attractive.

"Oh." Jo burned with curiosity as she stared at the ring. It must weigh two carats. Why was he carrying it? Her writer's mind teemed with questions. "She gave it back to you?"

"No." He looked surprised. "She never took it."

"I'm sorry." Jo looked away. She hadn't meant to pry such an embarrassing admission from the man.

"No, no. You don't understand," Rob said. "I never asked her. I chickened out, told her I couldn't see her anymore."

"Just like that, after you were about to marry her?" Jo asked, astonished.

Rob sighed. "It probably seemed that way to her, but I'd been worrying about this for months. Marriage seemed like the right thing, but I just couldn't go through with it."

"But didn't you love her?"

"Love her?" One heavy, black brow arched quizzically. "I'm not even sure I like her. Frances *should* be the perfect wife. She's polished, well bred, the kind of woman everyone expects me to marry. Unfortunately, we have nothing in common, no shared values. We don't enjoy talking with each other. There isn't even any chemistry, at least not on my side."

"Then why were you going to marry her?" Jo asked.

"Oh, you know." He shrugged as if it were obvious. "Family pressures."

Jo made a small sound of assent, but she didn't know. She couldn't imagine marrying to please your family. Of course, her family would never make such an unreasonable request, but if they did, she wouldn't hesitate to tell them to can it. She glanced at her

passenger. Asking prying personal questions
of a stranger was rude, but she couldn't help
it. She just had to know more. "What do *you*
want in a wife?"

"Companionship,   joint   decision-making,
love. And honesty," Rob answered. "I spend
all day playing games, dickering, and nego-
tiating. I don't want to have to do that
at home. Today was a perfect example.
I'd planned to take Frances to a quaint
little restaurant for lunch and propose to
her there, but she had already made reservations at the country club. Needless to
say, we never got around to lunch."

"You're not marrying her because you
couldn't agree on a restaurant?" Jo was
incredulous.

"Of course not." Rob frowned. "But it was
symptomatic of our whole relationship. We
never were on the same wavelength, and I
was usually the one who gave in."

"I see," Jo said, but she still didn't see,
not by a long shot. The whole thing sounded
bizarre, unbelievable—like something out of
a soap opera.

Rob must have sensed her reaction, because suddenly he chuckled. "What am I
doing, rambling on like this? You offered
me a ride, not a counseling session."

"I don't mind. I like to hear people's stories." She smiled, feeling a little uncomfortable about her reaction to this particular story. She liked to think she understood how

other people felt, but with Rob she didn't have a glimmer. She couldn't get the situation straight in her mind, much less how he must feel about it. "So, where were you headed when your car stopped?"

"Headed?" Rob looked blank. "Oh. I was on my way back to work, but if it's out of your way, you can just drop me anyplace that has a phone."

"Where do you work?"

"Valley Bank. The downtown Davenport branch."

Davenport was definitely out of her way. To get there, she would have to drive right by her nice, warm apartment, but Rob interested her. She wasn't ready to let him go quite yet. "I can take you. When do you need to be there?"

"I have a one o'clock meeting."

"Good, that's plenty of time, even in this weather. I do need to stop at the Kwik Stop and get some gas."

"That's fine with me. I could pick up a sandwich." The warmth of his smile made her feel delightfully feminine.

Snow had turned to rain by the time they drove into the little river town of LeClaire. The village had a good-sized residential district up on the hill, but the business district wasn't much—just a row of ancient brick buildings backed up to the river, filled with antique and craft shops that catered to tourists exploring the Great River Road. A bank, hardware store, and grocery sat across the street, and the drugstore sported an old-time soda fountain. Except for the streetlights, the town hadn't changed much since Mark Twain's day.

Jo drove through town and pulled into the Kwik Stop. "I'll just be a minute," she said, turning off the motor and hopping out of the car.

"No hurry," Rob answered. He stared at her back for a long minute before opening his door.

She sure was cute. Those sparkling big eyes flecked green and brown reminded him of new grass peeking through spring-warm earth. Wavy, walnut-brown hair down to her shoulders and a saucy, upturned nose completed the picture. With that coat covering her, he could tell only that her figure was slim.

Definitely interesting. Rob felt a twinge of guilt at the trend of his thoughts, but he shrugged them off. Frances hadn't been his idea. He had been pushed into dating her, pushed toward marriage. It was a good thing for both of them that he'd come to his senses in time.

Whistling, he walked into the store. He grabbed a tuna sandwich, poured two coffees, and paid for Jo's gas.

When he got back to the car, she had the hood up. He thought of giving her a hand, then remembered that he hadn't even checked his gas gauge. She couldn't possibly know less about internal-combustion engines than he did.

"I got us both some coffee," he called.

"Thanks!" Her voice was muffled by the hood.

She headed for the shop when she was finished, so Rob took the opportunity to study her vehicle. It was the ugliest thing he'd seen in a while. A station wagon, at least fifteen years old, it was an awful olive green. He grimaced. At least it ran.

Since she was still in the Kwik Stop, he glanced at the pile of books and papers on the front seat. A couple of reference-type books, a notepad, a few typewritten letters. Feeling like a burglar, he thumbed through the letters until he found one with her name and address at the top.

He pulled out his address book and scribbled in her address. As he replaced her papers, he chuckled under his breath. So she lived in LeClaire. Taking him to Davenport was fifteen miles out of her way. He couldn't imagine why she was doing it, but it made his life easier. He was glad he'd bought her gas, though. Come to think of it, he was glad his car had quit when she was about to come down the road. And he was delighted that he'd broken off his dead-end relationship with Frances. For the first time in ages, he felt free.

Jo frowned at him as she climbed back into the car. "You didn't have to pay for my gas," she said.

"I know." He handed her a cup of coffee.

"Passing the favor along when you had the chance would have been enough."

"I'll do that too."

She pressed her lips together as she started the car. "Well, I could have taken care of it. I'm not a charity case, you know. I may not drive a Mercedes, but there's nothing wrong with my car."

"No one said there was." Rob grinned. So she was proud. And stubborn, or she would have dropped the subject after her first snide remark. She was probably short of cash too, or she wouldn't be prickly about such a small gift.

Her independence tickled him. And that accent! Her "I's" all came out like "ah's," "well" became "way-ell," and "you know" blended into one word—"y'know." He wanted to ask her some questions, just to hear more of the delightful way she murdered the English language. So he did.

"Where are you from, Jo?"

"Texas." The frown that lingered from their confrontation over the gas seemed less fierce as she added, "And Oklahoma."

"Texas *and* Oklahoma? How can that be?"

That made her frown disappear altogether. "My dad works in the oilfields, so I've lived here and there."

"Iowa is a long way from Texas. What brings you to the Quad-Cities?"

She stopped at a red light on the outskirts of Davenport and smiled at him. "You sure do ask a lot of questions."

"Just being friendly." He shrugged, shaking a few drops of water off his beaver coat. He should have worn a raincoat.

"I'm writing a book about riverboat gambling."

"Oh, yes, the world's greatest tourist trap." Rob snorted at the idea, but then the rest of what she'd said sank in. "You look awfully young to be a writer."

"I'm old enough. So what about you? What do you do at the bank?"

"I'm a vice president."

"Speaking of young, you're a pretty young vice president." Her eyes sparkled as she smiled at him.

"A pretty minor one too," he admitted with a laugh. "I work in the trust department."

"Do you like working in a bank?"

"It helps pay for my Mercedes," he joked. From the way she rolled her eyes, he suspected she didn't entirely approve of that answer. He was still trying to think of some way to redeem himself when she stopped in front of the bank.

"Well, here you are." Her bright smile gave no hint that she was sorry to see him go.

Rob tried to think of something clever to say, but nothing came. "Thanks for the ride."

He held out his hand, and her expression softened as she took it.

"Y'all take care now," she drawled. Their eyes met for a long, intense moment; then he was out of the car, standing on the slushy sidewalk, and she was driving away.

He fingered the address book in his pocket as he watched her go.

Chapter Two

U P FROM THE GRAVE. Jo gnawed on her lower lip as she stared at the computer screen. That wasn't a bad title for her introduction. She put her hands on the keyboard and started typing:

If you had asked most observers a few years ago, they would have told you riverboat gambling on the Mississippi River was as dead as Tom Sawyer and Indian Joe. Yet today proud stern-wheelers once again ply the muddy waters, and plush salons are filled with the jingle of coins, the dealers' calls.

No, it's not quite the same as it was in Mark Twain's day. Massive diesel engines now power the paddle-wheels, and it is the boats' owners who rake in the profits, not the individual dealers. Yet some things never change. The sharp, metallic scent of coins, the twang of banjos, the rush of excitement when your number comes up. . . .

Once started, the words came easily. Except to take a sip of water from the glass beside her, she didn't stir until the sun was setting.

Her legs and back were stiff when she finally stood up. She glanced out her picture window at the muddy shadows spreading over the river. After two weeks of research, putting words on paper felt great. She supposed she should have finished her research first, but the need to turn what she was learning into a story was too strong.

After her run-in with Joseph Porter, she deserved a little treat. Besides, she needed to get her mind off the other Porter she had met today. Rob.

She stretched and walked into the kitchen to make coffee—decaf, she decided with regret. Regular tasted better, but she needed her rest. Her mother had always teased her about how much she slept. Mom got by cheerfully on four hours a night, and Jo's four brothers did too. Only Jo and her dad needed a full night's sleep.

She wondered what her father would think of Rob. Not much, probably. She could almost hear him, his voice scratchy from too many years of smoking. "What a stuffed shirt! Can't even fix a car. Probably gets those muscles from lifting weights."

Jo giggled as she poured water into the coffeemaker. That was his ultimate insult. In her father's opinion, working out at a gym lacked the character-building qualities of "real" work.

Knowing that some of her dad's ideas were outmoded, she also knew she had accepted them at some basic level. Consciously, she believed running a bank or a big corporation was just as necessary as farming or working on an oil rig, but she couldn't quite imagine a man who didn't come home from work with dirt under his fingernails.

Still, she liked Rob, despite the fact that he seemed strange to her. He had been polite, and he'd been able to laugh at himself over his car. He was a bit stubborn, but that made him more appealing, not less. Stubbornness was a trait her dad and her four brothers had taught her to associate with the male of the species. She grinned. People had called *her* stubborn from time to time, but she wasn't, not really. She just knew what she wanted.

Yes, Rob was interesting. Her family would give her a hard time if she brought a man like him home, but their teasing would be of the good-natured variety. They all had hearts as big as Texas, and once they realized that she was serious, they would accept him despite his oddities.

Would Rob's family be as generous with the woman he eventually chose? From what he had said, she doubted it.

Shrugging, she poured herself a cup of coffee. Rob's family problems weren't her concern, and yet she hadn't been able to get them, or him, off her mind. He had been there as she sorted through her notes, as she made a ham sandwich for lunch.

Only writing had driven him out of her head, and apparently he hadn't gone very far even then, because he was back the minute she took her hands off the keyboard. She almost wished she were working tonight, so she wouldn't have time to think of him. Dealing blackjack was the perfect antidote to a wandering mind.

Jo was just sitting down on the old sofa that had come with the apartment when there was a knock at the door. She approached it warily. Who could it be? She hadn't been in town long enough to make many friends. She wished the old wooden door had a peephole.

Slipping the chain lock into place, she opened the door a crack and peeked around it.

"Rob!" Jo blinked and wondered whether thinking about him had somehow made him appear, but she immediately discarded the idea. He was too big, too solid, to be an apparition. "What are you doing here?"

He smiled crookedly. "Invite me in, and I'll tell you."

"Oh, of course." She slipped the chain off the door and opened it.

"At the risk of sounding bossy again, I'm glad to see that you're careful about opening your door to strangers."

Jo chuckled. "Not very careful. I just let you in."

Rob looked confused, but then he laughed too. "I guess I don't see myself as a dangerous character."

"Let me get you a cup of coffee, and you can tell me why you're here. And how you found me," she added.

As she poured his coffee, she smiled. Rob might not consider himself dangerous, but that depended on how you defined dangerous. He had managed to invade her thoughts all day, hadn't he? When she walked back into the living room, he was studying her apartment with interest.

She tried to see her place through his eyes. There were three rooms: a kitchen, living room, and bedroom. It must seem pretty rundown to a banker. Chipped ivory paint covered the walls, and the floor sported a worn brown rug. The cheery, pink-flowered throw she had bought didn't hide the couch's sag, and her two oil paintings of the Mississippi, although good, were by an unknown artist. At least the place was spotless.

Rob didn't look repulsed by his surroundings, just amazed. Jo smiled. "Amazed" and "confused" seemed to be his two most common expressions. That didn't surprise her. If she found him strange, it stood to reason that he felt the same way about her. So why was he here?

"How did you know where I live?"

"I, uh. . . ." Rob's face turned red. "I saw your address in that pile of papers you left on the front seat."

Jo grinned, amused at a sudden mental picture of Rob rifling through her papers, jotting down her address. "Snooping through people's papers isn't a very dignified thing for a banker to do."

"Oh, I don't know. A banker needs plenty of information to do his job."

"Right." Jo rolled her eyes, but she couldn't help feeling flattered. He must have wanted to see her again. "Let me take your coat."

He had exchanged the soggy fur for a sensible raincoat. Minus the wet fur scent, he smelled good, like an expensive blend of citrus and sandalwood. And he really was big, six-two or three, with a linebacker's broad shoulders. He looked both attractive and formidable in his gray suit and tie.

Suddenly shy, Jo looked down and asked, "So, what can I do for you?"

"Go to dinner with me."

"Dinner?" She giggled nervously, then wished she had managed to hold her reaction inside. Being asked out hadn't shocked her so much since Bobby Hammond invited her to the eighth-grade dance. "Why would you want to go to dinner with me?"

"Why?" That seemed to stump him for a minute. "I thought it would be a nice way to thank you for helping me out this morning.

I made my meeting on time and had time to take that ring back to the jeweler. I don't even think I caught a cold."

So he hadn't changed his mind about Frances. Irrationally, Jo was pleased. But the idea that he was simply paying a debt with a meal didn't please her. For a minute she had thought—hoped—he just plain wanted to see her again. "Look, I appreciate the offer, but you don't have to—"

"But I want to," he said, cutting off her protest. "Eating alone is no fun. Please say you'll have dinner with me, Jo." He laid a hand on her shoulder, and she melted.

"All right, but I have to change clothes." She glanced at his expensive suit, then down at her scruffy jeans.

"Just wear something warm," he advised. "It's cold out there. If you don't mind, I'll use your phone to make a reservation while you change."

"Go right ahead. I'll be only a few minutes."

Jo closed her bedroom door and yanked the closet door open. Panic time. She pulled an oversized, gray-green sweater out of the closet and held it up in front of her. The mirrored door confirmed that the color brought out the green in her eyes. Its bulk gave her slim figure a little more shape too.

Gray cords would have gone well with the sweater, but Rob was making a *reservation*. That meant he was taking her somewhere fancy. She rolled her eyes. What could you expect of a banker? She settled on a calf-length black skirt whose gathers made it seem as if she had real hips, heavy gray cable-knit tights, and a pair of low-heeled shoes. Her hair and makeup took only a minute; then she sprayed cologne on her throat and wrists.

Rob had poured himself another cup of coffee and was studying her computer when she opened the bedroom door. He turned at the sound. "Nice outfit," he said with a smile.

"Thanks."

"So this is where you write." He glanced at the computer again. "Do you write anything besides histories?"

"Anything that pays money. I've done a few magazine articles and four mystery novels. My pen name is Jo Crystal. Right now the riverboat-gambling book is my big project. I rented this apartment for its view of the river." Rob grinned at that, and Jo decided that he was relieved to hear she had some logical explanation for living in such a dump.

"You're a full-time writer, then?" he asked.

"Not yet. I still have to supplement my income with a little honest work. I'm combining research and making money by working as a blackjack dealer at the moment."

Rob choked on his coffee. "A blackjack dealer?"

Jo drew herself up to her full five feet seven inches. "Do you have a problem with that?"

He shook his head, but he didn't answer until he caught his breath. "Not really. I guess I'm just surprised."

"Do you know of a better way to find out what it's like?"

"No," he said, "but . . . you seem too young to be a dealer. How old did you say you were?"

"I didn't." She tried to frown at him, but she couldn't quite manage it. "But I'm twenty-six."

"I knew you couldn't be very old," he said with satisfaction. "You also seem too soft and sweet for that kind of work." As if to illustrate his point, he reached out and brushed back a strand of hair that had fallen forward, letting his fingers graze her cheek.

His touch was gentle, unthreatening. Jo liked the feel of his fingers, but his assumptions didn't please her. "I may look soft outside, but I'm tough as an old shoe inside."

"I'll just bet you are." Rob looked skeptical as he moved away. Jo felt a pang of disappointment. For a moment there, she had thought he was going to kiss her. Not that she would have wanted him to. She hardly knew him. Still, he could have tried.

Half irritated, she folded her arms across her chest. "And what makes you such an expert judge of people? Your advanced age? I'll bet you're all of twenty-five."

"I'm twenty-seven," he said, in a tone that said she should be impressed. "And I think you're about as tough as a marshmallow.

You probably take in every stray cat you find."

Jo smiled guiltily and wondered if he'd noticed the bowl of milk on the back balcony. It wasn't her fault the kitten had showed up the day after she moved in. "Are we going to dinner or not?"

"Yes, and we'd better get going. I made our reservations for six-thirty, and we have to drive to Princeton."

Princeton. That was a relief. Although she had heard there were a couple of good restaurants in the little river town five miles north of LeClaire, none of them looked too fancy from the outside.

"I see your car is working," Jo commented as Rob helped her into the red Mercedes.

"You were right." He cleared his throat. "It was out of gas."

It wasn't easy to refrain from laughing. "This is a nice car. I didn't know banking paid so well."

"Well . . . it makes a difference if your daddy owns the bank. I assumed you knew that, since you've been researching the area's history."

Jo stared at him, openmouthed. "I do. It just didn't register—Porter is such a common name. Edward Porter ran a string of riverboats, and his son Frank founded Valley Bank," she recited. "It's one of the few banks in the area that made it through the Depression without collapsing."

"Right. And I'm Robert Edward Porter, the Third. Old Edward was my great-great-grandfather, and I'm named for him. So is my dad. They skipped using the name for a couple of generations, so he's a 'second,' not a 'junior.'"

Jo laughed weakly. "I'm overwhelmed. I didn't realize I was going out with a member of Davenport's elite."

"Don't be. I'm pretty ordinary."

Ordinary? She let her eyes glide over his broad chest and wavy black hair. Just looking at him made her feel small and feminine. And he was rich, old-money rich—at least by Midwest standards. He must be considered the catch of the century among the country-club set. No wonder she couldn't relate to him, or he to her. They were as different as sheep and goats.

They arrived at the restaurant before Jo could pursue that thought. It was a nice place but unpretentious, with stuffed bass on the walls and a picture window showcasing the river. Just like her apartment, but not as shabby. The waiter seated them right by the window.

"This won't be too cold for you, will it?" Rob asked with a concern that Jo found charming.

"No, it's wonderful."

"You know, I've read a couple of Jo Crystal books."

"Oh?" Jo held her breath. She didn't dare

ask if he had liked them. What if he thought they were awful? Criticism from total strangers hurt, and already Rob was no stranger. His opinion mattered to her.

"I'm a big mystery fan. Your plots are complicated, but I like that. The one where the woman is accused of murdering her husband was great. I never did figure out who did it, but when I looked back, the clues were all there."

"*Maid for Murder?* I liked that one too. It's my latest book."

"I'll have to read the others, if I can find them. Paperbacks don't stay in print long."

"I have copies, if you're really interested," Jo said shyly.

"I am! Maybe you could autograph them for me." He reached across the table and took her hand, enveloping her fingers in warmth. A nice sense of security spread through her. That seemed strange to Jo. Between her family's regular moves, and having to compete with four other kids for her parents' attention, she had learned early to rely on herself. Drawing such comfort from another person seemed odd.

"You must have started writing young."

She nodded. "I've always written. I sold my first short story when I was sixteen, and my career has been developing slowly since then."

The waitress appeared and took their orders. Rob chose the catfish that was a fixture on every Iowa menu, while Jo ordered steak, cooked medium rare.

"You're going to be difficult, I see," Rob said.

"What do you mean?" Jo blinked. What had she done wrong?

"What kind of wine goes with fish *and* steak?"

"You don't need to worry about wine for me. I'll just have a beer and decaf coffee."

"No wine with dinner?" Rob's eyebrows shot up as if he'd never heard of such a thing. He smiled at the waitress, who stood patiently by the table. "I'll have coffee too, the regular kind. And why don't you bring us a bottle of dry champagne, with two glasses?"

"You want the coffees after dinner?" the waitress asked.

Jo shook her head. "Now, please." After the waitress left, she frowned at Rob. She might have known someone with his background would have rules about what you should drink with your dinner. "I really don't care for most wines, Rob."

"You may like this one," he said with a smile. "Tasting it won't hurt you."

"Dry means sour," she pointed out, "and the only sour I like is Chinese hot-and-sour soup."

"We'll see." He grinned as if he had a secret and switched subjects. "Starting your career so young must not have left much time for other things in your life."

"Such as?"

"Oh, I don't know." He shrugged. "Men, school. . . ."

Jo studied him, suddenly suspicious. What was the point of all these questions? To make certain she was the "right kind of woman," like Frances had been? If he had to ask, she wasn't. Her eyes narrowed and her smile felt brittle. "Oh, I made time for men. Just never found one worth keeping."

"What about school?" Rob repeated.

The waitress brought their drinks, opening the wine bottle and pouring a small amount into Rob's glass. Jo watched with interest, despite her irritation with his nosy questions. She had seen the ritual plenty of times—at a nearby table in a restaurant or on television, but she'd never been involved before. Rob tasted, then nodded to the waitress. At least he wasn't pretentious about it.

She could tell he was still waiting for an answer to his question. "Everyone's not like your family, Rob. Two kids in college is about all a family like mine can afford, and I have four brothers."

"So you gave up your chance at an education to help your brothers."

She bristled at the disapproval in his voice. "That's not true! Except for English, my grades weren't all that good. Donnie and Brad are B-plus students."

He didn't say anything, but he still looked skeptical. Jo knew she shouldn't care. She didn't need to justify her life choices to anyone. Nonetheless, she found herself saying, "I'm getting there in my own good time, anyway. Between community-college classes at night and correspondence courses, I should have my associate degree next year." If she didn't flunk that correspondence course in algebra.

"I wasn't criticizing, Jo." Rob squeezed her hand. "It's just that you seem so bright, and you're such a good writer. You deserve a chance to develop your talents too."

Put that way, it didn't sound so bad. Rob's tone wasn't condescending, either. Maybe she was being oversensitive. "I couldn't have handled four straight years of school, anyway," she said in a calmer voice. "I wanted to get out and *do* things, find out what life was all about."

"I can relate to that." Rob chuckled as he uncorked the wine bottle and filled his glass. He poured a scant inch into the bottom of her glass. "I didn't make it through in one sitting, either. Too restless."

"Really? What happened?" She never would have guessed that Rob had been restless. He seemed so stable, so directed.

"I dropped out my junior year and spent about ten months bumming around Europe."

Europe. Jo's eyes widened. "What did your parents think of that?"

"They had a fit, but I wasn't around to hear

most of it." He grinned. "I was studying at Columbia, you see, and I met this girl. She was going to Europe that fall because she'd been promised a small part in a movie. I was in love, so I decided to go with her. That was the spring of my sophomore year. By fall her job had fallen through and I didn't love her anymore, but I was still in love with the idea of Europe.

"I let my parents think I was going back to school, sold my car, and signed on as crew on a tramp steamer. My parents found out when the dean called them. It was the second week of school, and I'd never registered."

"They must have been worried sick."

His smile faded. "I'm sure, but that never occurred to me at the time. Luckily, my letter arrived a day or two after they found out. Then they were just furious."

"What did they do?" Jo asked, amused and slightly shocked. It was hard to imagine Rob doing something wild and crazy.

"What *could* they do?" He shrugged. "Wrote me nasty letters, shouted at me when I called home. Threatened to disown me." He grinned again. "Threatened to break my neck. When I finally ran out of money and asked them to rescue me, they sent me an airline ticket. Mom told me later that they figured if they sent cash, I'd probably head for India. They got even, though. I finished college at a state school."

Jo couldn't help laughing at his story, but

her amusement was tinged with a certain sadness. True, they had both rebelled, both asserted their independence. The same urge must have driven them. But how different was the way they had expressed that urge.

Europe! One of her life's goals had been a matter of youthful rebellion for Rob. She stifled a sigh.

Rob didn't seem to notice her melancholy. "Now, taste your wine," he said.

She pushed aside her dreary thoughts, braced herself, and took a sip. Blinking, she sipped again, then drank the rest. "Why, that's not sour at all."

"Don't ask me why, but in champagne, 'dry' means semisweet. 'Brut' is dry. Do you want a glass?"

She nodded, and he filled her glass. The rest of the meal was good, their conversation pleasant, but even the wine couldn't induce her to lower her guard.

Rob was good company, polite and interesting, but he could have come from another planet, for all she understood him. Every time she felt herself warming to him, she reminded herself that they came from different worlds.

She assumed they would leave after dinner, but Rob led her into the lounge instead. After ordering Irish coffees, hers made with decaf, he asked her to dance.

"Can you do a two-step?" she asked doubtfully. "It's the only dance I know."

"Don't worry," he said. "Just follow me, and you'll be fine."

The band was playing a rhumba as Rob led her onto the dance floor. He slipped his hand around her waist and pulled her close, but she had trouble relaxing. The way he held her was awfully intimate, and what if she stepped on his toes? She followed his steps stiffly, feeling clumsy.

She was relieved when the song finally ended. Rob stopped near one edge of the dance floor. One hand still around her waist, he leaned over and whispered, "I don't bite, Jo. I promise."

Her cheeks stung with embarrassment. Was it so obvious that he made her nervous? "I told you I don't dance very well."

"Sure you do. You just need to relax." He pulled her even closer as the next song started. She started to stiffen as unaccustomed warmth flooded her, then decided she was being silly. Dancing close was *supposed* to be pleasant.

Refusing to feel guilty because she enjoyed his touch, she moved closer. His closeness made it easier to follow the steps, and soon she was enjoying herself. She was glad he didn't try to make conversation while they danced. That would have been too complicated.

It was after midnight when he walked her up the stairs to her apartment. She felt flushed and excited from the dancing, the wine, and Rob's presence. Her heart pounded as she wondered whether he would kiss her.

For a minute she thought he was just going to say good night and go, but then his arm slipped around her shoulders and his lips came down on hers. His kiss was gentle, his lips warm. They made her feel warm too—warm and tingly and pleasantly female. She had just settled her arms around his neck when he broke the kiss and straightened up.

"Well, tomorrow is a workday. I'll call you soon." As she walked inside, he added, "Be sure to lock your door."

Jo slipped the chain into place, then hurried to her bedroom window. Pulling back the curtain, she watched the red Mercedes drive off.

She frowned as she straightened the curtain. Strange as he was, she liked him. She liked his gentleness and his sense of humor and the way he felt in her arms.

But she wasn't going to see him again, even if he did call. What good would it do? Everyone knew that sheep and goats don't mix.

Chapter Three

Wind howled across the parking lot. The big red and white riverboat tugged at its moorings as if it wanted to get out of the wind too. Jo hurried across the lot, wound her way through the crowd of tourists waiting for the next "cruise," and flashed her employee I.D. at the guard.

She hardly paused long enough for him to nod at her. Once aboard, she took the elevator down to the lowest level and slipped into the employees' dressing room.

Tossing her purse into her locker, she pulled her costume out of her gym bag and shook it out. Holly Sands, a cocktail waitress and the first friend she'd made in Davenport, already sat in front of the mirror, penciling black eyeliner around her huge, green eyes.

Jo frowned at her. "Holly, you're putting that on way too heavy. You'll look like a redheaded geisha."

Holly grinned in the mirror. "That's easy for you to say. Your lashes are so dark, you don't need makeup, but some of us aren't so lucky."

"With all the cleavage that costume exposes, the fellas won't notice your eyes, anyway." Jo smiled as she exchanged her jeans and sweater for a high-necked white blouse and long, black-satin skirt. Dealers' tips weren't as good as the waitresses', but Jo thought hers was the better job because she got to wear real clothes, instead of the skimpy uniforms the waitresses wore. The black bow tie choked her, and the green visor had a tendency to droop, but nothing was perfect. "Help me with my hair, will you?"

"Sure." Holly fastened Jo's hair in a neat ponytail, fluffed her bangs, and helped her pin the visor in place. "Where were you last night? Edison wanted you to work, but you weren't home."

"I went out to dinner."

Holly's eyes widened. "With a man?"

"Of course with a man," Jo retorted, vaguely irritated by Holly's surprise. She'd be the first to admit that Holly was prettier than she, but she *had* been the Junior Miss

Roundup in third grade.

"Don't get all bristly, Jo. You just moved here. I didn't know you'd had time to meet anyone."

"I just met him," Jo admitted, mollified.

"Do you like him?"

"Yes, but he's not exactly my type. I doubt if I'll see him again."

"You could date him until you find someone better."

"That wouldn't be honest," Jo objected. "Besides, what if I started liking him too much?"

"Oh, Jo!" Holly laughed. "You worry too much. With an attitude like that, you'll never have any dates."

Jo didn't argue. Holly had her own opinions about men, and nothing would change them. They talked about the weather as they headed for their stations.

Her blackjack table was empty, but Jo expected that. The management cleared the boat of passengers after each "cruise" and charged the next group of gamblers admission. *Then* they let them play the tables and machines—and took their money in earnest.

Jo snorted as she filled the shoe with cards. The whole operation was tailor-made to separate the unwary from their money. Even the cruises were a sham. The riverboat never went more than a mile or two from the docks, and in the winter it didn't move at all. It just sat there, surrounded by thin, dangerous ice, raking in the money in four-hour shifts.

The *Iowa Lady* was a pretty boat, though. Automatically she glanced around. Industrial-grade carpet that aped the design of an expensive Persian rug, red-and-white flocked wallpaper, fringed red-velvet drapes. Everything else was gilt and mirrors. Even the members of the country band on the stage were dressed like old-time gamblers.

The tables shone like emeralds in the sea of red, and the slots, now still and silent, tinkled and flashed gaily when the customers arrived. Upstairs, a lavish buffet sported an ice sculpture and an astonishing array of food, and the drinks in the lounge all seemed to come with umbrellas. Rather like an amusement park for grown-ups.

It was a fun place to work—but not forever.

Once the doors opened, there was no more time for reflection. The deck was filled with movement and laughter, and Jo contributed her share.

The shift passed quickly. As she drove home, her body ached with exhaustion, but that was to be expected after nine hours on her feet, with only a half-hour break. The other nights weren't as bad, because then she only worked the moonlight cruise, from nine to two A.M., instead of starting at five as she did on Tuesdays. And she had Saturday,

Sunday, and Monday off.

She was so tired when she fell into bed that she didn't even think about Robert Porter. Well, not much, anyway.

Rob frowned at the pile of paperwork on his desk. That was what he hated about going out of town. No one touched a thing while he was gone. They just let it pile up.

With a weary sigh he flipped through the stack. Three long, confused letters from rich old ladies who had decided that their estate plans were all wrong, half a dozen sets of documents that, with his approval, would create new trusts. Twice that many packets from lawyers. As head of the trust department, he often served as the executor of clients' estates. And phone messages galore, all requiring callbacks. Actually, no one else could have handled any of it.

He glanced at his watch and sighed again. The whole day had slipped away while he put out fires. That left him with his regular work untouched.

He had a choice. He could order a pizza and spend the evening catching up on his paperwork, or he could make good use of his season basketball tickets. It should be a great game, Iowa against Illinois, and his sister and brother-in-law weren't going. If he stayed at the bank, four good seats would go to waste. He grimaced. The work would wait.

He began straightening his desk, then paused. Going to a game alone wasn't much fun. Maybe he should ask Jo Christenson to go with him, if she was still speaking to him. He grinned ruefully. She had been on his mind off and on since he took her to dinner a full week ago. He had intended to call her over the weekend, but then John Hartlieb had called. He needed some advice on his investments in Florida.

Rob snorted as he rummaged through his pocket, looking for his address book. Mostly, John had wanted a golf partner for the weekend. They had left late Wednesday and hadn't made it back to the Quad-Cities until Sunday night.

He supposed he should be glad to have a job that included four-day golf outings. He was, most of the time, but Hartlieb's lectures on how to make a fortune in the hardware business got old.

And sudden, disconcerting images of sparkly hazel eyes had played havoc with his golf game. He'd almost called her from Florida, but that had seemed excessive. After all, they hardly knew each other.

Ah, there it was. He pulled the booklet out of his pocket and flipped to her address, smiling as he remembered her surprise when he showed up on her doorstep. It seemed longer than a week since he'd seen her. Had he waited too long? He reached for the phone, then paused.

It was already close to four. Maybe Jo wouldn't appreciate a last-minute invitation. Would she consider it an insult? He might do better to call and invite her out Friday night, but he wanted to see her now.

He picked up the receiver and dialed. Funny. His heart had never pounded like this when he called Frances.

Jo turned from her computer with a sigh. She'd been writing since before eight A.M. In fact, the whole weekend had been productive. Maybe she would get the next chapter started before she returned to work on Tuesday.

The only thing that had slowed her down was a hint of depression because Rob hadn't called.

The river glistened under the pale, wintry sun as Jo stared pensively out the window. Even now, with bare trees stretching their branches skyward, the water heavy and gray and the tourists gone south for the winter, it was a moving sight. The old riverboat bobbed at its moorings, and a stray dog poked list-lessly around the landing. Looking for dis-carded trash fish, no doubt.

Discarded. That was how she felt. It was silly, but she had half believed she would hear from him. No matter that she told herself she wouldn't have gone out with him again, it would have been nice to have the chance to turn him down. Or maybe she would have ignored her common sense and said yes.

But that would have been stupid. He was so stable and conventional. He didn't under-stand her; she had seen it in his eyes. And she didn't have a clue to the inner workings of his mind. He'd probably figured out that they had nothing in common and decided to save himself some trouble.

Sighing, she pushed all thoughts of wavy black hair, intense eyes, and broad shoulders out of her mind and turned back to her computer. She moved the cursor to the top of her outline for Chapter Three and typed in, THIEVES AND CUTTHROATS: LIFE ON THE MISSISSIPPI. That chapter title seemed a bit dramatic for a nonfiction book, but she left it for the time being.

She hit the "print" key and stood up. Enough for one day. After stacking the printed pages and shutting down the computer, she headed for her tiny kitchen. It was time to wash the few dishes she had dirtied during the day and decide what to have for dinner. She filled the sink with soapy water and started scrubbing.

The telephone shrilled. She glanced at the wall phone and let it ring. Could it be Rob? Her heartbeat sped up a bit, but she shook her head.

More likely it was Holly. She'd gone out with her friend once and decided she didn't enjoy Holly's idea of fun. Barhopping just wasn't her thing. Holly had been hinting that they should do it again, though, and it would be hard to turn her down.

The phone kept ringing. Jo hesitated. What if it *was* Rob? She shook soapsuds off of her hands and snatched the phone.

"Jo Christenson."

No one spoke for a moment, and she wondered if the line was dead. Then a warm male voice spoke. "At least I got the right number. I was beginning to wonder."

The voice was familiar. Could it be? Jo stared at the receiver. "Who is this?" she asked, suddenly hopeful.

A low chuckle dispelled her doubts. "This is Rob Porter. Don't tell me you've forgotten me already."

"Oh, no, but I was beginning to think you'd forgotten me," she admitted, then wished she'd kept quiet instead of letting him know she'd been thinking of him. Her brothers always seemed to prefer the women who kept them guessing, but Jo wasn't much of a game player.

"No way would I forget you," Rob answered. "I'd have called sooner, but I've been out of town since Wednesday. I got back late last night."

"Sounds hectic," Jo said, smiling. So he'd been out of town. That explained why he hadn't called. And he had thought of her while he was gone! "What's up?"

"Not much. Uh . . . ." He cleared his throat. He seemed to be stalling. As if he were nervous, Jo realized with surprise. She wouldn't have thought anything would make him nervous. "Look, Jo, I know this is really short notice. If you say no, I'll understand."

"What did you have in mind?" she asked.

The silence stretched uncomfortably before

he spoke. "There's a University of Iowa basketball game at seven-thirty tonight. They're playing Illinois, so it should be pretty good. Would you like to go?"

"You want me to go to a basketball game with you?" Jo chuckled. He'd seemed so worried, she hadn't known what to expect.

"If you don't want to go . . . ." He sounded offended.

"No, no. I'd love to," she assured him, still smiling. "You just surprised me."

She could hear his relieved sigh. "Great. I'm about done here. Why don't I pick you up around four-thirty? We can get a snack on the way, then have dinner afterward."

"Eat twice? That seems rather excessive," Jo teased.

"Watching basketball is hard work, and I wouldn't want you to go home hungry. You're already thin enough."

A pleased tingle spiraled up Jo's spine at the approval in his voice. "Okay. I'll see you then."

The dishes disappeared in record time; then she dashed into the bathroom and ran a hot bath. Glancing at the clock on the counter, she scowled. This would have to be quick.

Minutes later, wet hair spilling over her shoulders, Jo peered into her closet. What should she wear to a basketball game with a banker? Something feminine yet practical. And it should be slightly sexy.

Not like that vest Holly wore the other

night. Jo giggled at the memory. The vest had been cut halfway to her friend's navel. She was surprised Holly hadn't caught cold wearing it.

No, she didn't want to come out looking like Holly, but she did want to look . . . kissable. She chewed her lower lip thoughtfully and pulled a long-sleeved sweater in a soft, grayed rose out of her drawer. It would do nicely. The soft cashmere was eminently huggable. A gray corduroy skirt and black boots completed her outfit.

She hurried to the bathroom to dry her hair, added a touch of rose to her cheeks and eyelids, sprayed on a light floral perfume, and she was ready. Then she returned to the living room to await Rob's arrival.

A tentative knock sounded at the door before she sat down. She hurried to open it, feeling breathless with excitement.

"Hi." She tried to sound casual and sophisticated but didn't quite carry it off.

"Hello. Sorry I'm—" Rob broke off in midsentence and stared at her.

Jo blushed under his gaze. Had she forgotten to button something? Surely not. Then why was he looking at her like that? She wanted to ask, but her voice wouldn't come.

Rob finally nodded. "Well, don't you look pretty tonight! Actually, you always do. I'd just forgotten how much I like looking at you."

"Thank you," she said shyly. The extravagant compliment seemed to demand more of a response, but she couldn't think of any, so she changed the subject. "If you're ready, maybe we should go."

He nodded, but when he helped her put on her coat, she noticed that he managed to run his fingers along her cashmere-covered arms. She must have made a good choice.

His obvious approval made her a little nervous, but by the time they'd picked up sandwiches and soft drinks and hit the freeway, she was able to ignore her discomfort enough to make small talk. Rob was easy to talk to, and soon they were exchanging stories about their respective weeks like old friends.

The lots nearest Carver-Hawkeye arena were already jammed, so they parked several blocks away and walked to the stadium. The team was already filing onto the court by the time they found their seats.

"We barely made it." Jo fidgeted as Rob's arm settled over her shoulders. The bucket seats in the Mercedes had given her plenty of space, but these seats were so close that Rob's leg brushed hers every time she moved. She tried to sit still.

Rob didn't seem to notice her problem. "Looks like the stadium is about full tonight."

"Except for those seats right beside us," Jo pointed out.

"My sister, Paula, and her husband have season tickets too, but today's her birthday and she wanted to go dancing." Rob chuckled. "Bill hates to dance."

"But Paula loves it?"

"So she says, but she's not a natural dancer like you. I think she makes Bill take her to prove that he loves her."

Jo's cheeks glowed with pleasure. She had never considered herself a good dancer, but she had found a new confidence in Rob's arms. "You make it easy," she said softly.

The tip-off cut their conversation short, and once the action began, Rob seemed more interested in the game than in her. Jo was both relieved and irritated. Relieved that she wouldn't have to field any more of his sophisticated flattery, irritated that he hardly knew she was there.

That wasn't quite right, though. He did lean over now and then to explain a fine point or comment on a particular player, and he squeezed her shoulder affectionately every time an Iowa player made a good shot. Still, it was a good thing Jo understood basketball. Rob was too engrossed to explain the whole game to her.

Although the game started out well, Illinois took the lead midway through the first half, and the Hawkeyes never caught up. They trailed by ten points at the half; the game ended with the Hawks down sixteen. Jo clung to Rob's arm to keep from losing him as the disappointed crowd surged out of the stadium. "I'm sorry they lost."

Rob shrugged and slipped a hand around her waist. "It happens. Maybe dinner will be better."

By the time he pulled the Mercedes out of the parking lot, the only restaurant without a long line was a twenty-four-hour diner out on the highway. He grimaced as they settled into a corner booth. "I'm sorry about this. I planned to take you someplace nice, but I didn't consider the crowds. We're usually here early enough to park close."

"You take off early for basketball games?" Jo asked, surprised.

He grinned. "Sure. Some things are too important to miss."

She nodded, but his answer confused her. In her world it was work that was important, and you stayed until you'd put in your hours. She'd never heard of leaving early to go have fun and wasn't sure she approved. Who took care of business while the privileged few were out amusing themselves? She didn't voice her thoughts, though. Criticizing her host's way of doing things would be downright rude.

She didn't understand his apology about the restaurant, either. It seemed like a nice enough place, with cute, checked curtains at the windows and silk flowers on the tables. "What's wrong with this restaurant? It's cute, and I'll bet the food will be great. Besides, the company's wonderful."

"Thank you." To Jo's delight, Rob blushed. So he wasn't quite as blasé as he liked to appear. He captured her hand across the table, his fingers closing over hers possessively.

"You know, Jo, I haven't enjoyed a game so much in years."

"Even though your team lost?" she teased.

"That's right," he admitted, grinning.

She returned his smile. It was nice to know he'd enjoyed her company, even if he *had* seemed more interested in the game than her. But basketball must mean a lot to him, to miss work for it. "You have season tickets. Do you go to every game?"

"Just about."

"Don't you get tired of it?"

He looked puzzled. "Why would I get tired of it?"

"Well, doing the same thing, week after week, year after year . . . ."

"But it's not the same," he objected. "Every game is different, and we go out to different restaurants afterward. Sometimes we go to away games and stay overnight."

"I see," she said, but she didn't. It all sounded the same to her. Watch the game, eat. While she tried to puzzle out his bland acceptance of the routine, she examined her menu. She had more luck with the menu than Rob's attitude. She just couldn't understand him.

The meal was good, though. As they walked out of the restaurant, Jo sighed with contentment. "That cherry pie was delicious. My skirt fit better before dinner."

"Oh?" Rob's hand on her shoulder halted her. He turned her to face him, pretending to study her.

"You look fine to me," he said with a broad smile. "Perfect, in fact."

Jo smiled, her cheeks hot.

The drive back to LeClaire was pleasant, although Rob was quiet. Jo was glad, because she didn't quite know what to say to him. Finally he pulled up in front of her apartment.

"It was a lovely evening, even though Iowa lost." Jo twisted her leather gloves. Why did Rob make her so nervous? It must be because they were so different. She was never sure how to act, couldn't tell whether his smooth compliments were polite conversation or his honest feelings. That was one reason she shouldn't be here with him. She refused to think about all the other reasons.

Her nervousness increased as he walked her up the stairs. What if he wanted to kiss her again? What if he wanted to come in? Just the idea made her hands shake. He was so charming, so dangerous. Letting him close to her was inviting heartbreak.

"Well, good night." Jo fumbled with her keys until the worn lock clicked. The door swung open, spilling light into the hallway.

"Wait!" Rob caught her arm. "When can I see you again?"

This was her chance. All she had to do was open her mouth and say "Never." Or she could put him off, then make excuses until he gave up. Instead, she found herself saying, "Why don't you come to dinner Saturday? I'll make Oriental food."

"Sounds great. What time?" His smile made her forget all the reasons she shouldn't encourage him.

"Say seven?" That would give her plenty of writing time during the day. And plenty of time to worry about the folly of seeing a man who was all wrong for her.

"Perfect. I'll bring the wine."

Jo shrugged off her worries for the moment. She'd already committed herself, after all. "Make sure you get some sake," she said.

"Sake? I thought you didn't like wine." His brown eyes sparkled with teasing light.

"Oriental food requires sake," Jo said firmly.

"If you say so. Now. . . ." He bent his head and brushed his lips against hers.

His kiss was so gentle, so tender. How could he make her feel so special with just a kiss?

Jo wrapped her arms around his neck and returned the caress, and Rob responded by dropping his hands to her waist and holding her closer. She didn't stop him, trusting him to know how far she was willing to go.

Her trust was rewarded when he raised his head and let her go. Perversely, she was disappointed that the kiss had ended so soon.

"Good night, Jo. I'll see you Saturday."

"Saturday," she repeated softly. She watched him walk down the old wooden stairs, then shut the door with a frown. Cooking dinner for Rob made about as much sense as putting a rabbit in a cage with a coyote.

Chapter Four

Rob poked listlessly at his poached egg. He should have gone running instead of mooching breakfast at his sister's house, but he'd hardly slept the last couple of nights for worrying about his date with Jo. Now it was almost on him and he was too nervous to do anything to relieve his tension. Besides, he'd had to deliver Paula's birthday present.

"Is there something wrong with that egg?" Paula snapped. The hot curlers in her dark-blond hair bobbed as she crossed her arms over her turquoise satin housecoat.

Rob glanced up without interest. "It's fine, Paula. I'm just not feeling like myself this morning."

"I was wondering why you showed up for breakfast."

52

"Didn't you like your birthday present? I thought turquoise was your favorite color."

"Of course I did. The necklace is beautiful, but it's not why you're here. You could have sent it home with Bill anytime." She poured a cup of coffee, adding a liberal dash of cream, and plopped down across the table. "What's wrong?"

"I'm not sure." With just two years separating them, Rob and Paula had always been close. They had shared secrets since they could talk and had always brought their dating problems to each other. Even so, Rob didn't know if he could talk about Jo with her.

It seemed almost like a betrayal. Besides, he really *wasn't* sure what was wrong. If he knew, he could have come up with a solution and slept better.

"Trouble at the bank?"

"No, nothing like that."

"Then it must be woman trouble."

"What else?" Rob chuckled ruefully. Trust Paula to cut right to the chase.

"Are you sorry you let Frances go?"

He scowled. "Hardly."

"Good. I never did like her, despite what Mom and Dad thought. But it's only been a couple of weeks. Surely you haven't got another one on the hook already?" Paula's eyes narrowed. "Tell me about her."

"Oh, all right." Rob acted as if he agreed only to please her, but he was relieved. He needed to talk to someone.

"Remember when my car broke down last week?"

"Oh, yes. Some girl picked you up and drove you to the bank."

"I took her to dinner that night, to say thank you."

"And you liked her," Paula supplied.

"Right. We went to the basketball game on your birthday too." He pushed his cold egg aside and sipped at his coffee. Why was it so hard to talk about Jo? Just thinking about her left him feeling confused.

"What's the problem? Did she dump you?"

He shook his head. "She's fixing me dinner tonight."

"Then what are you moping about? It sounds like things are moving along nicely."

"It may look that way, but they're not," he grumbled. "I just don't understand her."

"That's no surprise. You just met her. Give it time," Paula said in her most irritatingly reasonable voice. She poured more coffee and nibbled at a piece of dry toast as if nothing in the world were wrong.

Rob growled under his breath. "I don't think I have all that much time. This may be our last date if I don't do something drastic." He leaped to his feet and paced around the kitchen, feeling like a caged animal.

Paula didn't seem perturbed by his agitation. "What's her name?"

"Jo. Joanna Christenson."

"What's she like?"

He stopped pacing long enough to smile. "Pretty. Brown hair, brown eyes flecked with green. Fairly tall and slim. She's a writer, and she comes from Tex-as." He drew the word out as Jo had done.

Paula grinned. "Sounds charming, but I still don't see what you're worried about."

Rob drew his brows together and frowned. "It's not easy to explain. Jo is a little flaky. She moved here just to research some book she's working on, and she acts as if she may take off at any moment, intent on her next project. Besides, I get the feeling she doesn't think much of the idle rich."

"But you're not idle. You work harder than anyone I know," Paula pointed out.

Rob chuckled sourly. "That depends on your point of view. I'm sure she would see that if she gave me a chance, but. . . ."

"You're afraid she's going to ride out of town before you can lasso her."

"It's not funny, Paula. This is my life you're making jokes about," he said, scowling.

"Sorry." At least she had the decency to look guilty. "If it matters that much to you, you'll just have to come up with a gimmick to keep her around until she has a chance to see the real you."

Rob thought about Paula's suggestion all day. He considered it as he brought his personal books up to date, puzzled over it as he bought the sake Jo had suggested, and a decent bottle of burgundy, just in case.

He still didn't have any brilliant ideas when he left his house, a little after six.

Thunk, thunk, thunk! Jo brought the cleaver down across the steak with firm, precise strokes, dropping the slices into a dish of homemade teriyaki sauce.

She frowned at the dish. Somehow dinner had escalated into a major project. Her eyes wandered to the river outside her kitchen window. Some diehard fishermen were launching a johnboat, despite the fact that a thin sheet of ice already clung to the riverbank. They looked foolish, bundled up against the cold, as foolish as she felt about getting carried away over Rob. She'd tried to keep things casual, but he was already too important to her.

What was so special about the man? He was good-looking, but so what? The world was full of attractive men. There was his size, that gentle strength that made her long for the safety of his arms. But those strong, safe arms were what she needed protection from. She couldn't afford to fall in love with Rob.

Jo set down her knife and counted off the reasons.

One. He was rich. Rich men seldom had their priorities straight. They thought they could buy whatever they wanted, and she wasn't for sale. Two. He was pushy. They'd been out twice, and twice he had told her what to do. Granted, he'd never asked her to do anything that wasn't in her best interest, but she still didn't like it. Three. He clearly had a rigid, unbending view of life. Even if she could forgive his other faults, she couldn't take that. She needed a man's respect and approval, and a vagabond wife wouldn't meet with Rob's approval, that much was sure.

She sighed and headed for the bedroom, where she slipped into tan cords and a high-necked, moss-green sweater that picked up the green flecks in her eyes. Tying her hair back with a ribbon, she decided against makeup, then stroked on a touch of eye-shadow, anyway. There was no harm in looking nice.

It was a good thing she was nervous enough to be ready early, because Rob knocked on her door a few minutes before seven.

She tried to look severe as she let him in. "You're early."

"So I am." He smiled sheepishly as he glanced at his expensive wristwatch. "Actually, I'm punctual by nature."

"That figures," Jo said with a resigned smile. Just one more point of difference. They were miles apart in every way. So why did his arrival make her feel like singing? "I'm never on time for anything."

"How do you make it to work?" he asked, drawing his eyebrows together.

"My bedroom clock is set fifteen minutes fast." That seemed to confuse him, so she asked, "Do you want a glass of wine before dinner?"

"Sure. Let's have the burgundy and save the sake for dinner." He handed her a brown paper bag.

Jo suspected that he just wanted to put off trying something new, but she didn't say so. Maybe he'd be more receptive to the sake after a glass of burgundy. She brought out two glasses and the wine and curled up at the far end of the couch, feet tucked under her. "You get to help cook, you know," she said.

"I do?"

"That's right." He looked so amazed that she couldn't help but smile.

"Well, all right, but I warn you, I'm not much of a cook. I never really learned how."

"What do you do for food, then? Eat out all the time?" Suddenly Jo had a horrible thought. Surely he didn't still live at home.

He seemed to hesitate. "I do eat out a lot, but Gretta cooks for me when I'm home. She's my housekeeper," he added.

Jo's mouth dropped open. She couldn't help it. "You mean you don't even pick up after yourself?"

"I'm a very busy man." He sounded defensive. "I make my own breakfast, and I'm gone at lunch, so she only fixes supper."

Jo forced a laugh. She hadn't meant to offend a guest in her house, but he'd caught her off guard. Some of the wildcatters she'd met in Texas and Oklahoma were pretty well off, but she'd never known one who had a housekeeper. Maybe a twice-a-week cleaning lady, but not a real housekeeper. And none of them cut their days short so they could attend a ball game, either.

"You don't have to explain," she said. "Having household help isn't a crime. I was just surprised, that's all. This should be a real adventure for you, then. Shall we get started?"

"Sure." Rob followed her to the kitchen.

"You can fry the egg rolls. Just make sure they don't get too brown." She filled wonton and egg roll wrappers, some with pork and vegetables, others with a sinfully rich mixture of crab and cream cheese. Plugging in the deep fryer, she explained, "Wait till the light goes off. Put the goodies in with these tongs and take them out when they're golden brown."

Rob hadn't been kidding when he said he couldn't cook, but he was a good sport, clowning around with the tongs, asking questions as she stir-fried the main course, and stealing raw snow peas and carrot strips.

"Hey, these are hot!" He dropped the egg roll he'd just bit into and took a sip of his wine. "I burned my tongue!"

"What did you expect?" Jo asked, laughing. "You just took it out of a pot of boiling oil. And you're about to burn the rest of them."

"Sorry." Rob fished the egg rolls out and set them in the paper-towel-lined bowl, just a bit too brown. Then he dropped two more egg rolls into the oil. "Aren't we making a lot of these things? We won't have room for dinner."

"Speak for yourself," Jo retorted. "I haven't eaten all day." She didn't add that she'd been too nervous about seeing him to eat.

Dinner was an unqualified success. Despite his worries about too much food, Rob ate his share of appetizers, finished his hot-and-sour soup, and took a second helping of stir-fry.

He even liked the sake. She had expected him to turn up his nose at the unusual flavor, but he'd sniffed, then sipped the sample she poured him, nodded, and let her fill his glass.

He even tried the glazed bananas, although he didn't seem thrilled with them. They were too sweet for Jo too, but it wasn't dinner without dessert, and they were the only traditional Oriental dessert she knew how to make.

Maybe she had misjudged him. She still couldn't see him jumping onto every bandwagon that came by, but perhaps he wasn't completely set in his ways. Maybe their relationship had a chance, after all.

"That was wonderful," Rob said, taking a final sip of his sake. "Much better than they serve in any of the local places. I'm surprised some man hasn't married you on the strength of your cooking alone."

Jo laughed easily, realizing that he was just teasing. "The problem is, I don't cook very often. Usually it's salads, fast food, or frozen dinners."

"I knew there had to be a catch." He shook his head and smiled.

Although he offered to help with the dishes, Jo insisted that they leave them. If he had no more experience with dishes than with cooking, her few pieces of good china were safer with sweet-and-sour sauce drying on them.

They played a couple of games of Scrabble, which Jo won handily.

"I should have known better than to play Scrabble with a writer," he grumbled, but his smile gave him away. She could tell that he wasn't one of those men who hate to lose to a woman.

Then they sat on the sofa, hand in hand, and shared another cup of tea. She couldn't remember a more pleasant evening with a man.

"It's getting late," he finally said. "I'd better be on my way, but would you like to go to dinner sometime this week?"

Jo braced herself. This was the time to tell him he was wasting his time, that they weren't right for each other. But what if she was wrong? What if they did have a chance at finding love?

Rob had just proved that he wasn't the rigid, unbending man she had expected. Her feelings for him were special, different from anything she had experienced before. And the more she knew about him, the stronger the attraction grew.

She tried to imagine herself as a banker's wife, living in a fancy house on a hill. Wearing expensive warm-up suits to shop for designer clothes, playing bridge with the ladies to while away the long, boring afternoons.

No, it would never work. They were just too different.

"I'm pretty busy during the week," she said with regret.

"This weekend, then." Obviously he'd missed her gentle hint.

"I'm going to be tied up." Jo hoped she sounded firm. Surely he'd get the message.

His eyebrows drew together. For a long, tense moment Jo was afraid he would argue with her. *Please don't make this any harder,* she thought.

He seemed to hear her silent plea because his face cleared. "I see." He smiled and leaned back against the old sofa, putting a little extra space between them.

So he'd understood her subtle message. Instead of the expected surge of relief, Jo felt like crying. In a minute he would stand up and walk out of her life and she wouldn't stop him. She didn't dare.

"Working two jobs must keep you pretty busy."

Eyes down, Jo nodded.

"And I'll bet finding information on Davenport's history isn't easy. Most people don't care about the past."

"That's true," Jo agreed. She raised her eyes, wondering where this conversation was heading. Just moments ago Rob had been trying to arrange a date; now he was calmly discussing her work. She felt a little hurt that he'd given up so easily. "I've been having a terrible time getting anything useful. Not many people keep old diaries and things anymore, and the few I've read aren't very helpful."

"What about the special collections at the library?"

"They have some good sources, but I'm still searching for something to make my book stand out."

"That's too bad." Rob's smile didn't seem particularly sympathetic. An uneasy prickle crept along her spine. What was he up to?

"I'm sure I'll eventually find what I need," she said.

"You know, I have some old journals in my attic. Maybe they would help."

Jo blinked in surprise. Then excitement took over. The Porters had been in Davenport forever, and Edward Porter had owned riverboats! But she was probably getting carried away. Everything she had tried so far had turned into a dead end. "Do you know how old they are?"

"Not really, but there are three trunks full of stuff. My house has been in the family for generations, and they looked ancient when I was a kid."

"They're probably worth looking at," Jo decided. "If you don't mind seeing all your family secrets in print."

Rob shrugged. "Knowing my family, I can't imagine that you'll find any skeletons in our closet. As far as I can tell, the Porters have been boringly proper since the beginning of time. Still, the journals might give you some new insights. Why don't you come over Tuesday and take a look?"

"No, I go to work early on Tuesday. How about Friday?" She would be recovered from Tuesday's long shift by then.

"Perfect. Come early and I'll get you started. We'll go to dinner afterward." Rob stood quickly and gave her a brief, affectionate kiss. Then he hurried out the door and down the stairs.

Jo was so excited, it wasn't until she climbed into bed and turned out the light that she realized he had tricked her. He'd wangled another date, over her objections.

That must explain his final triumphant grin, the way he had whistled as he walked down the dark stairway.

She supposed she should be irritated, but she just couldn't manage it. She really did want to see him again, even if it wasn't a smart thing to do. Besides, he was in for a surprise. Since she worked nine to two on Fridays, their "date" would be a short one. She drifted off to sleep with a smile on her lips.

Chapter Five

It was snowing when Jo let herself out of her apartment Friday morning. With the temperature hovering around zero, the flakes were more like tiny ice crystals than the heavy, white globes of slush that sometimes covered Oklahoma and Texas, but they were still snow. And they were beautiful.

She snuggled deeper into her down jacket, smiling. Winter up north promised to be fun. The thought made her pause. How much of her enthusiasm was due to the weather, how much to Rob?

She didn't want to think about it, didn't want to remember the way a certain tall banker's kisses made her tingle all over. Refused to consider how she would feel when their brief interlude ended. Because it would end. It was just a matter of time until their differences tore them apart.

But maybe she was looking at it wrong. Why not enjoy the way he made her feel special and cherished while she could? As long as she didn't let things go too far, her heart would be safe. That was risky, but it was clear that she couldn't just walk away. Maybe she should wait and see how things went.

Rob lived in the expensive, older Davenport neighborhood of McClellan Heights. Built on a hill overlooking the Mississippi, most of the houses had stood for a century or more, and some predated the city itself. It was easy to see how the area had picked up the nickname "Mortgage Hill." Who could build houses like that without taking out nice, fat mortgages?

Rob's house was one of the oldest in the area, a two-story red-brick affair with a broad, screened porch running all around the house and a sleeping porch above. Huge oaks shaded the lot, and the landscaping was formal.

Jo laughed ruefully. No wonder he had a housekeeper. He probably had a gardener as well. She wished she hadn't criticized him in her mind about it. Keeping up a place like that would be a full-time job.

He met her at the door, in a black three-piece suit that made his shoulders look a mile wide. His smooth self-assurance was even more evident now. Dressed for his world, a world that excluded Jo, he seemed intimidating.

"Hi." Suddenly shy, she glanced away.

"Good morning, beautiful." Rob grinned down at her as he wrapped an arm around her shoulders and pulled her into the foyer. "You're right on time."

"I didn't want to make you late for work." She wasn't about to admit that she'd been so nervous, she'd actually arrived early. She'd driven all over the neighborhood before ringing his bell.

"You can make me late anytime. Would you like some coffee?"

"Thank you," she mumbled. What was wrong with her? Why was she suddenly tongue-tied? This was the same man she'd teased about his cooking last week, the one she'd beaten at Scrabble. There was absolutely nothing to be afraid of, just because he had his "work clothes" on. She took a deep breath, and her nervousness subsided. "If you'll point me in the right direction, I won't keep you."

"Are you trying to get rid of me?" Rob asked, arching an eyebrow as he poured her a cup of coffee.

"Of course not. I was just—" She stopped. That was exactly what she'd been trying to do. "I do prefer to work by myself," she admitted.

"No problem. I have a morning meeting at the bank, anyway. Gretta took the day off to visit relatives downriver, so you'll have the place to yourself. I'll just show you where the trunks are and get out of your hair."

Rob led her up a broad staircase with an elegant cherry banister, and turned left down a long hall. Thick wool carpet in a blue floral print muted their footsteps. The design looked old, but the carpet itself was new.

"This is pretty." Jo gestured toward the carpet.

"Thanks. My sister picked it out. The hall was covered with hideous red carpet when my grandfather lived here."

"What happened to him?"

"He moved into a luxury condo when Grandma died." Rob stopped at the end of the hall. "Ah, here we are."

Jo watched as he pulled a key out of his pocket and unlocked a narrow door. A chill traced along her backbone as the door squeaked open, but she shook the feeling off. It was only an attic. A flip of a switch revealed a steep flight of wooden stairs illuminated by a single light bulb. The upper floor was shrouded in darkness. As he led her up the steps, Jo had to duck cobwebs and dodge ancient ice skates piled on the stairway. Several shoeboxes stuffed with yellowed receipts overflowed onto the steps.

"I don't keep the attic as clean as the rest of the place," Rob apologized.

"Why do you keep it locked?" Jo asked, sneezing as a cloud of dust rose around them.

"Habit, I guess. Granddad always locked it, to keep the kids away from the attic windows, I suppose. At least there's plenty of light." He wandered around the attic, pulling chains. Half a dozen bare bulbs sprang to life, revealing broken furniture, discarded toys, and more cobwebs. "We Porters don't like to throw things out. We get too attached."

"No kidding." Jo sneezed again as she wondered if they felt that way about the people in their lives. Did they value friends and family as much as they did possessions?

"I'd better open a couple of windows, or would that make it too cold up here?"

The concern in his eyes warmed her heart. The rest of her didn't need any warming, because the attic was hot and stuffy. "Go ahead. If it gets too cool, I'll close them."

"Just be careful. It's a long way to the ground." Rob opened two windows, one at each end of the attic.

"I know how to shut windows without falling out," Jo said crossly. Rob might be thoughtful, but he was also bossy.

"Of course you do." He moved close and patted her shoulder. "I didn't mean to sound like a mother hen."

"Well, you do sometimes." She tried to glare at him, but it was impossible with those big brown eyes gazing down at her. A reluctant smile came to her lips.

"I'll try to watch it," he promised, running his hands up and down her arms.

His eyes fastened on her lips, and Jo's eyes drifted shut in anticipation. It was about time he kissed her.

His lips brushed hers, so gently that she was hardly sure he'd kissed her. She leaned into his arms, but he only gave her one more quick kiss before he drew away.

She swallowed an unreasonable pang of disappointment. She hadn't come here for kisses, anyway.

Stepping over to three ancient-looking steamer trunks stacked against the wall, he nudged the closest one with a toe. "These are the trunks I told you about. They're mostly full of clothes, but at least one of them has some old diaries and account books at the bottom."

"Great," she said. "You'd better let me open them, or you'll get filthy."

He glanced down at his suit as if he'd just remembered he was wearing it. "Good point. I'll leave you, then. There's food in the refrigerator. Help yourself to lunch."

"Good-bye," she said, tilting her face up hopefully. Surely he wouldn't leave without a kiss.

"See you tonight." He gave her another brief, sweet kiss and strode out of the attic.

Jo sighed. He could have been a little more enthusiastic about that good-bye kiss. She wouldn't have minded a bit. Of course, every kiss made her long for another, made her more vulnerable to his charm. And she didn't want that, did she? With another long-suffering sigh, she found a worn footstool and set it in front of the trunks. Time to go to work.

By noon all Jo had managed to do was plow through a few flowery love letters and get herself covered with dirt. She was sneezing regularly, and her hands were black and grimy. Washing them at the kitchen sink felt wonderful. Her eyes widened when she opened the refrigerator. Rob had told her there was food but hadn't mentioned that he'd made lunch for her. The top shelf held a tray with her name on it.

Carrying the tray to the table, she opened the foil-covered dishes and chuckled. He was a sneaky one, all right. Shrimp, fresh strawberries, and chocolate cake were calculated to win her heart. It was a far cry from her usual cheese sandwich, but she thought she could adjust.

She finished everything on her tray with relish and washed up her few dishes. He'd probably scold her for that, but why should she leave a mess for Gretta? When she headed back upstairs, it was hard to pin her mind down. Her thoughts kept wandering from her work to the house's owner.

The fact that she had found nothing of interest made it hard to concentrate too. Maybe she was going about the project wrong. Instead of returning to the half-empty trunk she'd been digging through, she opened the other two. This time she refused to be distracted by any one item as she sorted everything into three piles.

One pile held clothes and miscellaneous keepsakes. The second consisted of letters, the third, diaries and account books. It wasn't easy to keep a firm rein on her curiosity, but she didn't pause to read anything. Some of the musty dresses and complicated undergarments practically begged to be tried on, but she resisted the urge. She was too old to play dress-up—at least until she finished her work.

She had all three trunks sorted in an hour, then repacked the useless stuff, more or less in the same trunks she'd found it in. When she was finished, two trunks were completely filled, and the third was half full. At least she knew how big a job lay before her.

Next, she sorted her finds by date. The letters were all in their envelopes, so they were easy to put in order. She was delighted to find that the oldest bore postmarks as far back as 1850. Others were newer—some as recent as the 1930s.

The journals were a little more complicated, because their dates overlapped. That wasn't too surprising, since they seemed to be written by different people. Their contents were different too. Some seemed to be diaries, while others contained facts and figures. Jo thumbed through the twenty-some handwritten volumes, but all that did was give her another sneezing fit. She'd have to sort the books too.

Three volumes of diaries in a feminine hand went into one stack. A quick glance at the bookplate in front of one book told her they had been written by Edward Porter's young wife, Marie. Jo knew Edward had been nearly forty when he married a girl not yet out of her teens. The diaries would probably be interesting, but not useful for her purposes. She couldn't believe that one young housewife's story would be much different from the accounts she'd already read.

There were some journals in a masculine hand too. One bore Edward Porter's bold, sprawling signature. His entries concerned his business, not his personal life. That was more what she had hoped for.

Finally there were the ledgers themselves. As Jo skimmed through them, she became more and more confused. There seemed to be more than one set of books, their dates overlapping. It took three times through the pile, but she finally got the volumes in order. Strange. There were two complete sets of books, one clearly marked Delta Enterprises. Edward Porter had signed or initialed most entries.

The second set of ledgers bore no markings on their covers, no signatures or initials, but the handwriting was Edward's. Maybe they were the household books, though normally Marie would have kept those. Jo opened one of the unmarked books at random. The first entry that caught her eye read: *May 22, 1889. Received 3 barrels whiskey, 2 barrels rum, 1 domestic brandy. Also 5 cases champagne, 2 x-grade brandy. Shipment short 2 cases cognac.*

That didn't sound like a household ledger, and the entry was dated ten years before his marriage. He might have had a house then, but he couldn't have used that much alcohol at home, not even for a party.

Jo flipped through the book until she came to a section marked Receipts. Edward Porter had been nothing if not efficient. Each date had entries marked Food, Drink, and Gaming. Occasionally there would be a fourth, unmarked entry. The largest dollar amounts always fell under Gaming, or were entered without description of any kind.

Odd. She'd understood that the gambling on the riverboats was private, not run by the "house." Since Edward owned the boats, he shouldn't have been involved in the card games. Had he been a gambler in his own right?

But the entries were too regular to cover an individual gambler's winnings. No gambling man, not even a crooked one, showed a profit every day.

Forgetting the dust that covered every surface, Jo leaned back against a trunk and stared at the book. Had Edward Porter run an illegal casino? It was possible, but it didn't fit with what she had read about him. And it didn't explain the blank entries. What could they mean?

She picked up one of the marked ledgers. It took only a few minutes for her to realize that these books covered the riverboats. Here, there were a dozen or more kinds of income, including Fares and Cargo. Gaming was conspicuously absent, there were no blank entries, and the items were identified by boat. Jo knew D.D. stood for *Delta Darling,* I.P. for *Iowa Princess.* There were others she didn't remember, but Edward Porter had operated five or six boats, so she assumed the other initials would match up to boat names.

That meant the other journals didn't concern the riverboats. He must have been involved in some kind of land-based business, and since she'd never seen it mentioned in the local histories, it must have been clandestine. That fit with the style of the journals, with their unmarked entries.

Jo turned back to the mysterious books and started at the beginning of the first volume. As she read, a strange feeling began to steal over her. These were no ordinary account books. They were too vague, too general. And why would anyone pay as much as Edward had paid for "security"? Bribes and payoffs were probably more like it. Keeping the police out of an illegal gambling operation would cost plenty.

She read on. *Had to get rid of Max today. Turns out he had a big mouth. Put the word out for a new guard.*

Questions and more questions. Jo didn't like the answers that kept coming to her. The Porter family had a fine reputation. All her sources agreed that the only blot on their spotless history was a little bootlegging during Prohibition, and that had been so common, it hardly counted.

She flipped another page and read the entry. *November 8. S. T. stopped by. Half now, half next week.* That didn't tell her much, but a week later there was a large, unmarked deposit.

Jo read on. *December 10, 1907. Contacted M. today. Not receptive, but he'll come around.*

Jo slammed the book closed, her head spinning. Come around? To what? And what did S. T.'s large, unmarked deposit mean? That almost sounded like some kind of blackmail or extortion. But it couldn't be. If Edward Porter had been involved in anything shady, someone would have discovered it before now.

Yet nothing else seemed to fit. The Gaming entries made it clear that he had made a lot of money from gambling. If he had really run an illegal casino, he would have had the perfect setup for a little blackmail.

There was a moment of shock; then the humor of it struck her. Just think—the prim, proper Porters involved in something shady.

Blackmail was a whole lot less funny than illegal gambling, but she wasn't sure about that part of it, and anyway, it was a long time ago.

What would Rob think when she told him? Her smile faded as she realized he might not share her amusement. Well, there was no reason to chance upsetting him before she'd read all the diaries. She could be completely wrong. She didn't really believe that, but it was best to check your facts before opening your mouth.

A glance at her watch told her it was almost five. Rob would soon be here to take her to dinner, and she was a mess. She took half a dozen of the most interesting-looking journals downstairs, then headed back to the second floor to find a place to wash up.

The upper hall was lined with family portraits. That didn't surprise her, but it was another indication of the gulf that separated them. The Christenson "family portraits" were Polaroids and snapshots, mostly unlabeled and stored in shoeboxes. Her mother brought them out on holidays, and her brothers were always ready to produce especially embarrassing shots to show to each other's dates. Only graduation and wedding pictures were formal.

She walked slowly along the picture-gallery hall, smiling as she recognized Rob's features in some of his ancestors' faces. The strong Porter cheekbones and heavy eyebrows were more attractive on the men than the women.

Not everyone looked like Rob, though. Besides a lone redhead and a couple of hooked noses that seemed to belong to another family entirely, there was a second Porter type that was almost as prevalent as Rob's type.

Those other Porters had sharp-featured, fine-boned faces, most with light hair and intelligent blue eyes. Although it was hard to tell from individual portraits, they looked fairly short.

Jo's smile faded as she stopped in front of a recent portrait. The man in the painting would seem almost petite next to Rob, and his hair was light brown, streaked with silver. He wore an expensive suit, and his blue eyes held no hint of a smile.

Jo's stomach tightened as she read the nameplate: *Joseph Porter. 1921——*. He was still alive. And if he wasn't the man who had run her out of his office a few weeks ago, she would turn in her computer!

Could this be Rob's grandfather? His age was right, and Rob had said that this had been his grandfather's house. Jo tried to ignore her next thought, but it came, anyway. If this had been Joseph Porter's house, the records she'd been reading were the ones he had forbidden her to use.

Jo tried to find a way around it as she washed up, but there was none. She would have to tell Rob about her meeting with his grandfather. She didn't look forward to it.

What if he wouldn't let her finish what she had started? Even worse, he might think she had deliberately lied to him. Frowning, she tried to figure out how to tell him.

Rob's arrival cut off her worries for the moment. He looked irritated when she told him she was too dirty for the nice restaurant he suggested, but a second look at her apparently convinced him. He was even less happy with her announcement that she had to be at work at nine.

"Couldn't you call in?"

"What would I tell Edison?" Jo asked. "That I can't come in because I have a date? I'm not going to lie to him."

"I suppose not." Rob's lips thinned. "But. . . ."

"We still have time to grab a hamburger and talk for a bit." Jo smiled, but his attitude bothered her. He acted as if her job didn't count. Granted, she wasn't a vice president of a bank, but her job was important too. To her, to the people who came to play the tables.

"No hamburgers." He looked as if he might argue with her some more, but then he shrugged. "I know a little Chinese place where we'll fit right in."

He helped her into the red Mercedes, then slipped in beside her. His hand was on the ignition when he looked over at her and smiled. "I shouldn't have suggested that you skip work for me. I'm just too used to setting my own hours, taking off when I feel like it, working late if necessary. I tend to forget other people don't have as much freedom."

Jo didn't say anything, she was too surprised, but she did reach over and squeeze his hand. That seemed to satisfy him, and she was happy when he kept hold of her hand.

Frank Wong's Chinese Deli wasn't a deli at all. On the slum side of the business district, it was filled with an odd mixture of derelicts and suited businessmen and women.

Once they were settled in the cracked plastic booth and the waiter had brought jasmine tea and egg rolls, Jo screwed up her courage. "I made some interesting discoveries today."

Rob raised his hand. "Please, Jo," he said, "we've both had a rough day, and we need to relax. I'll make you a deal. Don't ask me about my day at the bank, and I'll return the favor. You can tell me all about your research when you're through. Right now I want to concentrate on you."

"If that's what you want. . . ." Jo felt like a coward, but she was relieved too. If her work was going to come between them, putting off talking about it wasn't such a bad thing.

It was a pleasant evening. He held her hand as they shared stories about their friends and families and ate twice-cooked pork. Jo enjoyed his subtle, self-deprecating humor, but it was hard to work up much enthusiasm when he talked about what they could do together next summer. She had a sinking feeling that, for them, summer would never come.

When she got home, bathing, changing clothes, and rushing off to work left her no time to worry about Rob, but he was in her thoughts when she got back to the apartment around two-thirty, so much that she couldn't sleep. Finally she stopped trying and curled up on the sofa with the journals and letters she had brought home.

Rob had told her to take them, but she still felt like a thief. She doubted that he would go against his grandfather's wishes if he knew what they were, yet she couldn't resist reading the journals.

Knowing it was a weak excuse, she told herself that she should get all the facts before she upset Rob. Maybe she had jumped to the wrong conclusion about Edward Porter.

The journals provided only two more clues. The first read, *August 4, 1908. M. stopped in today. One week extension.* Then, one week later, *M. did not appear. Sent message.*

So M. didn't want to pay up. But what didn't he want to pay? Gambling debts? That would make sense, if it weren't for that other entry about M., the one about him "coming around." That hadn't sounded like a refer-ence to gambling. Still, she supposed it could be. Maybe Edward had been trying to get him to gamble on credit and he'd finally given in.

Thoughtfully, Jo turned to the letters. Most were love letters to Marie and her answers, correspondence with her family, and other personal mail. Some were different, though, their handwriting unfamiliar. A few had foreign postmarks. She set those aside. One letter had been posted with no return address. The handwriting was neat but masculine. Jo turned the envelope over in her hands. The postmark read, *August 15, 1908, Davenport, Iowa.* She pulled the letter out of its envelope.

Edward,

I beg your indulgence for just a few more days. I have funds coming in on the 31st to cover our agreement.

You know what the publicity would do to my career, and the shock would likely kill Rachel. If you don't care what you do to me, think of her and of your own good wife. How do you think Marie will feel to see her sister in such a position? For if I go down, the ladies will surely know who brought me to such an end.

Again, I beg you to have patience. Some things were never meant to be aired in the light of day.

James Martin

Jo wiped a hand across her burning eyes. Gambling debts, indeed. James Martin was a familiar name. He had been a local politician of some importance. Since he'd never been involved in any scandal, Jo could only assume that he'd come up with the money to cover their "agreement." She gave an unladylike snort. What a sad euphemism for blackmail!

It had to be blackmail. There was no other explanation for the cryptic entries and Martin's pleading letter. But what if she was wrong? A family's reputation was at stake. She couldn't afford to make a mistake. She picked up the journal. There, on the 31st, was an unmarked entry. The dollar amount was huge for the times. Edward had scrawled a line of explanation below: *M., finally.*

That tore it. Blackmail was the only logical explanation. Edward's ledgers indicated that his gambling parlor had been an elegant affair, so he must have attracted a wealthy clientele. He would have been in a perfect position to extract hush money from his clients, if he caught them doing something they didn't want broadcast. And a man well acquainted with the seamy side of life would be in a position to hear dirt about almost everyone.

That left two questions.

What had James Martin done that would be worth his career if the public discovered it?

More important, who else had Edward blackmailed? Jo picked up his journal and started reading again. Dawn was lighting the sky when she finally fell asleep on the sofa.

Chapter Six

"Jo, I've just discovered I have a little problem."

"What's the matter?" Jo's voice was steady
as she spoke into the phone, which was more
than she could say for her stomach. Rob's
words had caused a distinct knot to form
there. Had he finally found out about the
records in his attic?

After staying up most of Friday night, she
had slept Saturday away, but they spent
Sunday together, skiing at a small resort
near Dubuque. Well, Rob had skied. Jo had
spent most of her day sliding down frozen
hillsides on her rear end.

Rob had laughed when she indignantly an-
nounced that they didn't go in for such fool-
ishness where she came from. He'd made up

85

for it, though—first with dinner in an elegant old sandstone hotel, then with a moonlight cruise on Dubuque's gambling boat.

Research for her book, he'd called it. Jo *had* taken a few mental notes, but she'd had fun too. And she got her revenge for the way Rob had laughed at her.

Like the gentleman he was, he had insisted on providing her with a small stake for the evening's entertainment. She saw enough card games at work, so she headed for the slot machines—and won steadily. By the end of the evening she was three hundred and twenty-two dollars ahead, even after refunding Rob's forty dollars. Rob was a good sport, though he lost as steadily as she won. Jo's respect for him had grown.

Maybe that was why she put off telling him about her encounter with his grandfather. It would have been a shame to spoil the mood.

Waiting was a mistake, though. The longer she waited, the more difficult explaining would be, yet something had held her tongue. Perhaps she couldn't quite believe what she had discovered. Or maybe she was afraid she would lose Rob. Now it was Monday, and still the words wouldn't come.

"What is it, Rob?" she repeated nervously.

He sounded irritated. "I have to be out of town Saturday and Sunday. I'm golfing with a big client in Houston."

"Sounds like fun."

"But I wanted to see you this weekend."

"Why don't you stop by for a while Friday night before I go to work?"

"That's part of the problem. The yearly museum fund-raiser is Friday, and my sister is on the entertainment committee. I forgot all about it until she mentioned it today."

"I guess I'll see you next weekend, then." She bit her lip. Why did she feel so disappointed? It was only one weekend. Normally she liked spending time by herself. What was Rob doing to her?

"It's not that simple. I don't have a date for the dance. I figured I'd ask Frances, but that's obviously out. I was hoping you might go with me."

"Go with you?" Jo asked faintly. Surely Rob must know she had no experience with that kind of thing. Her idea of high society was a church potluck. "I don't think that's such a good idea. I really have a lot to do this weekend. Besides, I work on Fridays."

"I know, but I was hoping you could arrange to get it off or switch with someone. . . ." His voice trailed off. "I thought people in public-contact jobs sometimes did that."

"I suppose I could," she admitted reluctantly. "A couple of dealers owe me favors, but society parties really aren't my thing."

"If clothes are a problem, I'd be happy to take care of it."

Jo bristled at the suggestion that she didn't have anything to wear, even though it was true. "I can buy my own clothes, thank you.

Why don't you go alone? We can see each other when you get back."

"I can't go alone," he protested. "It wouldn't look right, and I promised my sister I'd be there."

"I . . . I guess you could take one of your other female friends." Now, why were those words so hard to say? She didn't want to be his one and only, or did she?

"I don't have any other women friends," he said firmly. "And I don't want any."

Jo smiled in spite of herself. His words made her feel so light, so happy. She waited for Rob to say something else, but he didn't. He wouldn't ask her again, wouldn't try to pressure her. His silence was more effective than any plea he could have made. She felt herself weakening. "Just how formal is this thing?"

"Black tie. The women will be wearing cocktail dresses or full evening gowns."

"That's no problem," Jo lied. "As long as you don't expect me to look like some society matron."

"Then you'll go?" He sounded like a kid with a new toy.

"I suppose so." She stifled a sigh and another smile.

"Great. I really appreciate this, Jo. I know you don't care for this kind of thing. Neither do I, to tell you the truth."

She drew her eyebrows together. "Then why are you going?"

"I don't have a choice. Besides the fact that Paula will kill me if I don't show, the bank has a reputation for supporting the arts."

"So this is part of your job?"

"Sort of."

"Like playing golf with clients?"

"Not exactly. It's not as important as maintaining contact with specific clients, but it's expected of me."

Jo tried to make sense of that and found she couldn't. Who ever heard of going to a party because it was expected? Parties were for fun, not work. "If you say so. I guess I'll see you Friday."

"Wait! You don't work tonight. What are you doing for dinner?"

"I'm busy, Rob." She smiled as she imagined his frown. He didn't like not getting his way. Neither did she, but as part of a big family, she'd learned to take it with good humor. He didn't have the hang of giving in gracefully.

"Am I allowed to ask what you're doing?"

"Sure." Jo knew she shouldn't tease him, but she couldn't resist. "I'm having dinner with someone else."

"Oh." He bit off the word. "You have the right, if that's what you want to do."

His hurt tone made her feel awful. She hadn't meant to bruise his feelings. "Don't you want to know who I'm having dinner with?" she asked.

"I'm not sure. Do I?"

"Uh-huh."

"All right." Now he sounded resigned. "Who are you having dinner with?"

"A little old lady named Annabelle Martin," Jo answered, strangely pleased at Rob's restrained show of jealousy. Jealous men usually irritated her, but with Rob it seemed like proof that he really cared about her, rather than mindless male pride of possession.

"Ah." His chuckle was filled with relief. "You had me going for a minute. Is she one of your research subjects?"

"Yes. She has a journal that belonged to her mother, and Annabelle is in her eighties."

"Sounds promising. I guess I'll see you Friday, then. Have a good time tonight."

"I'll try," Jo promised. "Y'all take care of yourself." She grinned as she hung up the phone. It was nice to know that he cared, and maybe she would have resolved the problem of his family records by Friday, so she could skip telling him about her meeting with his grandfather. She wouldn't have to say a word if she didn't use the Porter family records.

As she read the vague references to initials and odd sums, she had wondered again and again if she was reading more into the journal that it deserved. The illegal gambling she was sure of, but blackmail and murder. . . . It just seemed too farfetched. Maybe Edward Porter had simply fired Max, and M's plea could stem from embarrassment over gambling debts.

The only thing to do was get some corroborating evidence. If she couldn't, the journal wasn't enough on its own. And maybe she would discover some other, more acceptable explanation for the cryptic entries. James Martin's aging daughter was a good starting place. When she called the old lady, she hadn't been looking for a supper invitation, but Miss Martin had been adamant. Jo suspected she was lonely, and Jo didn't mind. She liked most old people.

Although it stood at the edge of McClellan Heights, the Martin home wasn't as big as Rob's house. A cozy-looking brick cottage with a moss-covered tile roof, it stood at the intersection of two winding lanes.

Miss Martin wasn't intimidating, either. White-haired and stooped with age, her watery blue eyes sparkled with excitement at having a visitor.

"Come right in," she gushed. "I've made us some tea."

"That's very nice of you, Miss Martin. I hope you didn't go to any trouble."

"Oh, it's no trouble, my dear. Dinner will be ready in a few minutes." The old lady hobbled off and returned with a sterling-silver tray and tea service.

Dinner was delicious, a light, flavorful cream-of-shrimp soup followed by tender braised chicken breasts and out-of-season asparagus. A delicate raspberry torte completed the meal. The menu surprised Jo. It was definitely not a typical Iowa meal.

Miss Martin wasn't your typical old lady, either. Because of the "Miss," Jo had assumed her hostess was a spinster, but Miss Martin explained that she had run a nursery school, "Miss Martin's Junior Academy." Rather than confuse her small pupils, she had kept her maiden name when she married.

"Though I used my husband's name socially, of course," she added. "Back then, I didn't really have a choice. When my husband died, I just stuck with Miss Martin."

The old lady had plenty of amusing stories, but she couldn't tell Jo much about the diary. She'd never been interested enough to read it when she was young, and now the faded ink was too much for her weak eyes.

It was nearly eight o'clock when Jo finally settled down with Rachel Martin's diary. She didn't mind the delay. The house was warm, the overstuffed furniture comfortable.

Feeling like an explorer at the edge of the known world, Jo opened the diary. It was after ten o'clock when she found what she'd been looking for. As she read, her heart sank.

March 20, 1909. Something is badly wrong. James is on a trip, and I opened the mail for him. Unless the county is wrong, our taxes are in arrears. How can that be?

April 2, 1909. I checked with the treasurer. No mistake—James has not paid the taxes. But I know there was enough money. Maybe it slipped his mind.

The next page was badly spotted with old water stains, but Jo managed to decipher most of it.

April 20, 1909. James arrived today. I almost wish he had stayed away. When I told him about the tax bill, he turned away from me. He promised to take care of everything and begged me to forget I'd seen it. Oh, I should have listened to him! But no, I had to know. Finally he told me.

Here, a line was crossed out, and the next few words were so blurred that Jo couldn't make them out.

. . . bribery. I can't believe it! I always thought he was so honest, so upright. That was what made me fall in love with him. Why would he do such a thing? He could have made it on his own. His cabs were the best in town without. . . . I can't say it.

I asked him about old Hank Jorgenson's horse-drawn carriage company—"Horses make a mess on the street," he muttered. "The city decided to ban them." When I asked if he had something to do with that, he looked away. I wonder what

*happened to Hank's family after they shut
him down.*

So James Martin had bribed someone on the
city council, intending to put his competitor out
of business. From what Jo knew of old-time poli-
tics, that wasn't unusual, but apparently Rachel
Martin hadn't agreed.

But where did Edward Porter fit in? She read
on. There were no more entries until May 28.
Jo's eyes filled with tears as she read.

> *I cannot believe he expects me to go through
> with this. After what that man has done
> to us, to think that my James will spend the
> rest of his life paying for one mistake. . . .*
>
> *And now James wants me to eat in his
> house, smile as if nothing is wrong. That my
> own brother-in-law could do this to James,
> to us, is unthinkable. If it were up to me,
> I wouldn't pay him off. I don't believe he
> would actually go to the newspaper with
> what he knows, if not for our sakes, then
> to spare his poor wife, Marie. I hardly see
> my sister lately, because I fear I'll blurt out
> the truth, and that would break her heart.
> I know it would. It has broken mine.*

Jo leaned back in her chair feeling sick. How
could one human being inflict such misery on
another? It was a struggle to make herself keep
reading.

* * *

*November 14, 1910. James won the elec-
tion. I suppose I should be glad. At least
we can pay the taxes and keep the house.
And, of course, keep up the payments for
Edward's silence. Yet, I cannot feel any joy.
I often wonder if he and Edward fixed the
election, the way he put Hank Jorgenson
out of business. And I think of what James
will do in Des Moines, when the legislature
is in session. Will he find another woman,
humiliate me further? He says he loves
me, but what are his words worth? He
has already proved himself a liar and a
cheat. I've thought of leaving, but there's little
Annabelle to consider. How could I care for a
baby alone? And a child needs her father.*

The rest of the diary revealed the story of
an increasingly embittered woman, suspicious
of everything and everyone. It was midnight
when Jo shut the book.

"Did you find what you needed, dear?" Miss
Martin asked.

"Yes, thank you." Jo forced a smile. "Sorry to
keep you up so late."

"You didn't keep me up. My movie won't be
finished for another hour. It's a John Wayne picture. Would you like to watch the rest with me?"

"Thanks, but I'd better get home. I have to get
up early tomorrow." Jo felt the old lady watching
her wistfully as she walked to her car.

Once home, Jo paced the apartment, haunted
by a growing sense of unease. Edward Porter a

blackmailer! And James Martin—he had been considered one of the good politicians, yet what he had done would put him behind bars if he did it today.

Jo knew she no longer had a choice. She had to talk to Rob, whether he wanted to listen or not. But how did you tell someone that his great-great-grandfather was a common criminal and you wanted to let the world know?

The upcoming dance didn't help, either. It was important to Rob, and she didn't want to spoil it for him. Yet, she couldn't stall much longer. How would he feel when he found out, first that she hadn't been entirely honest, then that the information he'd innocently turned over to her was so damaging to his family?

Of course, it happened a long time ago. Lots of families had infamous relatives. Her father had always sworn that his granddad ended up in Oklahoma because he'd been branded a horse thief in Massachusetts, and it was either flee or hang. He always laughed about the story, but Jo didn't think Rob would take a smear on the family name so lightly. And she suspected that Joseph Porter had known what was in the journals when he refused to let her read them.

She climbed into bed with a sigh. There was nothing to be done about it until next week. She couldn't ruin Rob's party with her revelation. Until then, she would just forget the whole mess and enjoy his company. She might as well—the dance might be their last date.

She was surprised when morning arrived. She hadn't thought she would be able to sleep, but she had, and soundly.

Pale wintry sun poured in her window, turning the off-white walls a pretty, buttery color. She felt surprisingly good, all things considered. As she walked into the living room, she frowned at her computer.

For once she didn't feel like writing. There was nothing to write until she talked to Rob, and besides, she needed to go shopping. It was a good thing she had won all that money on that gambling cruise Rob had taken her on the other night. Three hundred dollars wouldn't buy the kind of dress the other women would be wearing, but Jo had something those other women lacked. Ingenuity. She knew how to make do.

After a quick breakfast, she slipped on a sweater and jeans and a heavy coat and started her search. She began with the local outlet stores, but they didn't have what she wanted. She was almost glad. Now she could do some serious shopping.

But where? The local resale shops were out—too much chance of ending up with something from one of Rob's clients. Not that she would care, but she didn't want to embarrass him. That left vintage-clothing stores, sale racks in the better boutiques, and, as a last resort, fabric shops. Though she wasn't much of a seamstress, she could whip up a simple, long skirt in an afternoon.

She was halfway to her first stop when she realized she could squeeze in a little research too. A quick glance in the backseat assured her that she had a notebook, and her camera was always in her purse.

Her first stop was a vintage-clothing store in downtown Davenport. It was a fascinating place, cramped and colorful, full of the rich, musty scent of old silk. Traci, the owner, wore a bright-yellow fringed flapper dress, and she was happy to pose for a picture with one arm wrapped around a mannequin in a faded red saloon girl's gown.

Feeling that she had found a friend, Jo told her what she needed. She couldn't believe her luck when Traci produced a long, crushed-velvet skirt. The fabric was the deep burgundy color of old theater curtains, and it was cut so straight that walking would have been a problem if not for the slit up the right thigh. The waist was a bit loose, but a belt would take care of that.

None of the blouses Traci showed her seemed right. The styles were too old-fashioned, and they were all yellowed. Traci told her about Gypsy Rose, another vintage-clothing shop, down in Muscatine, though.

"It's worth the twenty-mile drive," she assured Jo.

After dropping her skirt off at the dry cleaner's, Jo took the river road to Muscatine. Gypsy Rose was more interesting than most museums. She spent a couple of hours prowling around, looking at everything, before she bought a long, hooded cape of black wool and an old cameo pin.

The pin was just costume jewelry, and the two together cost almost a hundred dollars, but she told herself that she could wear the cape with everything. And the cameo was beautiful, rose and ivory set in pewter filigree.

All she needed was a blouse and shoes. Shoes for her average feet wouldn't be a problem, so she checked her phone book for dress shops and headed back to Davenport.

Three hours and five stores later, she was discouraged. Who would have thought a white blouse would be so hard to find? Oh, she'd seen plenty, but they just weren't right—too plain or too fancy or too expensive.

She was on her way home when she saw the bridal shop. It wasn't much of a shop, in an older section of town, and The Blushing Bride was a boring name, but she was desperate. She stopped and pushed the door open.

"You look like you just lost your best friend," the clerk said with a smile. Blond and heavyset, her stretch jeans looked out of place beside the lacy bridal gowns.

Jo returned her smile. "I've been shopping all day, and my feet hurt," she admitted.

"What are you looking for?"

"A white blouse. Not just any blouse, the perfect blouse," Jo amended, laughing at the woman's incredulous look. She explained about the dance and the skirt she'd found and her budget constraints.

"I see what your problem is." The woman looked thoughtful. "And I may have a solution.

I don't handle many blouses, but about a year ago a gal came in here and ordered outfits for a wedding party. She wanted something nostalgic, so we went with long skirts and white blouses, sort of a Gay-Nineties look.

"She had them about paid for when she broke her engagement and ran off to Chile with a concert pianist. I still have a couple of the blouses, and the bride was about your size. I can give you a good deal on it."

The idea of wearing part of a bridal dress for Rob brought a rush of heat to Jo's cheeks, but she was desperate, and he would never know the difference. "Can I see it?"

She gasped when the woman brought out the blouse. It was white, all right, long-sleeved and high-necked, but it was sheer, just a wisp of white net. What kind of nut would get married in a thing like that? "I . . . I don't think so."

The clerk's ample bosom shook as she chuckled. "Oh, but you haven't seen the rest." She held up a white silk chemise, cut with broad shoulder straps and a sweetheart neckline. It was hand-beaded, with glowing seed pearls, crystal beads, and sparkling white sequins in a delicate rose pattern. "Want to try it on?"

Jo didn't need to try it on—she was already in love—but she did, anyway. It was perfect and fit as if it had been made for her. It would be just right with the burgundy skirt.

She walked out of the shop feeling as if she had stolen the blouse, but she refused to worry about it. The woman had seemed pleased to get rid of it, and Jo had cash left for shoes and a wide black belt. She was beginning to look forward to the dance.

"Come in. The door's unlocked." Jo hoped she didn't sound as nervous as she felt.

"Aren't you ready yet?" Rob called.

"Now I am." She walked out into the living room and stopped in shock. She hadn't been out with a man in a tuxedo since her high-school prom, and Jimmy McPherson would never be in Rob's league. The severe cut of the black jacket emphasized the broadness of his shoulders, while narrow trousers called attention to his long, lean legs. And, unlike Jimmy, he looked perfectly at ease. Jo felt like a poor relation in her patched-together outfit.

He was staring at her. Her cheeks burned as she realized she couldn't possibly compete with the kind of women he was used to. She wanted to sink through the floor.

"That's a gorgeous blouse, Jo. I've never seen anything like it."

She looked up cautiously—he seemed serious, so she managed a tentative smile. "Thank you."

"In fact, you look beautiful all over. I'll have to fight off the other men."

"Thanks. You look pretty nice yourself." She felt herself glowing. Maybe she wouldn't embarrass him, after all.

He helped her into her cape and escorted her to the car. On the way into town, he regaled her

with a story about his difficulties with a client—
a little old lady who came in every few months to
change her will. "This time she wanted to leave
it all to her cat. I finally sent her to a lawyer."

After a few minutes Jo almost forgot the fancy
clothes. He was the same man, and she was the
same too under the lace and pearls. Smiling to
herself about her fears, she told him about her
search for the perfect outfit.

Rob laughed when she listed the places she had
gone, and he finally reached over and squeezed
her hand. "Very resourceful. Of course, that
doesn't surprise me."

She beamed at the approval in his voice.

Lights and music spilled out into the snowy
night as elegant couples strolled toward the
museum. Rob's flashy auto had plenty of company here. The coatroom reeked of money too.
Jo had never seen so many fur coats in one place.
Her nervousness came back as Rob hung her cape
between a mink and what she suspected was a
silver-fox coat.

Then she remembered. Rob liked her simple
outfit. No one else mattered.

"Are they going to feed us?" she whispered
as they walked into the main hall. Now that
the worst of her stage fright had passed, her
appetite returned in full force.

"Just hors d'oeuvres. Didn't I tell you?"

She shook her head.

"Sorry. I thought you knew, or I'd have taken
you to dinner first." Rob slipped an arm around
her shoulders and pulled her up against him.

"Tell you what. We'll hit the buffet table first. If you're still hungry when we leave, we'll stop for some real food on the way home."

"Thanks." Jo smiled gratefully. Rob might not be perfect, but his ability to admit his mistakes made up for a lot.

The rest of the evening passed in a blur. After the first couple she met, Jim Somebody and a tall brunette named Catherine, the other guests blended into a confused tapestry of glowing colors and expensive jewels. Jo soon stopped trying to keep track of names.

At first she didn't know what to say. She didn't think her jaunts prowling waterfront pubs and shops in search of local color would interest them, and she couldn't follow their casual banter about racquetball and fashion, so she settled for smiling a lot and asking an occasional question.

That satisfied most of them. A few asked what she did and were impressed when she said she was a writer. Jo hid her amusement at the awe in their eyes. They wouldn't be so impressed if they knew what that meant—long days in dusty libraries, aching back muscles and strained eyes, odd jobs to cover the long stretches between sales. . . .

Jo liked Rob's sister. A petite blonde, she looked lovely in turquoise brocade. They chatted for a few minutes, and Jo found that Paula was as friendly and unpretentious as her brother. Paula's husband, Bill, was nice too, but he was a lousy dancer. She discovered that when he gallantly asked her to dance, then mashed her poor toes again and again. She was relieved that he didn't ask her for another dance. Her feet might not have survived it, and besides, she preferred the feel of Rob's arms around her.

Rob was pretty good about staying by her side, but he did get waylaid by a talkative client or friend now and then. When that happened, Jo would take a deep breath and strike up a conversation with the nearest available person. Most of them were nice, but all that smiling was a strain.

By midnight she was exhausted. The hors d'oeuvres weren't a real meal, and she had lost count of the glasses of champagne the white-coated waiters had pressed on her. One too many, from the feel of her temples.

Rob seemed to understand, because he studied her for a moment, then leaned close and whispered, "Had enough?"

"Too much, I think," she said, holding up an untouched glass of champagne. She leaned against him, grateful for his strong shoulder.

"Must be time to go, then." He started guiding her toward the door.

Jim Somebody stopped them on the way out. His date was nowhere in sight.

"What happened to Catherine?" Rob asked.

Jim scowled. "She split with some guy. Can you believe it?"

Rob grinned. "Tough luck."

"Easy for you to say, with this beauty on your arm." Something about his smile made Jo want to squirm. It was one of those slimy smiles that made a woman feel like a man could see right through her clothes. "I've been thinking, Jo," he said. "Don't I know you from somewhere?"

"Not unless you come from Amarillo or Tulsa." Her smile was cool.

Rob's arm tightened protectively around her shoulders. He and Jim exchanged a few more good-natured barbs; then Rob guided Jo out the door and helped her into the convertible.

They stopped at an all-night diner on the way home. Rob's eyes widened when she ordered a jumbo hamburger, fries, and a strawberry shake, but he didn't tease her about her appetite. He settled for pie and coffee.

It was a good thing he didn't expect brilliant conversation, because she couldn't have managed a witty remark if her future had depended on it. She was just too tired. That struck her as odd, because she usually worked later than this.

It must be the strain of meeting all those society types. Or maybe worrying about how to tell Rob that his great-great-grandfather was a murderer was getting to her. Perhaps she should just get it over with. She had her mouth open to tell him, but then she closed it. They'd had such a nice evening, it wasn't fair to spoil it for him. And if it was spoiled for her—well, that was her own fault. If she'd told him right away, she wouldn't have a problem.

She frowned. What was wrong with her? She'd always been the honest one, the one who 'fessed up when she did something wrong. Why couldn't she do it now?

Rob watched the stiff form beside him. What was wrong? The evening had gone beautifully. Jo had been a bit nervous at first, but she'd charmed everyone she met. She seemed to enjoy herself too, at least until now.

Maybe she was just tired. He decided not to push.

She still seemed quiet when they got to her apartment, so he made a special effort to let her know how much he was coming to care for her.

When he folded her into his arms, she rested her head against his chest, then looked up at him, her eyes wide, filled with such sweet trust that he had to swallow the lump in his throat before he could kiss her.

How could it feel so right to hold her in his arms? He had never experienced anything like it. And when he kissed her, the world around them ceased to exist, and there was only Jo, sweet and soft and giving. It was magic, pure magic.

As she slipped away from him and disappeared into her apartment, Rob fought the urge to grab her and pull her back into his arms, to kiss her until she admitted that she felt the magic too.

He glared at her closed door. They were so right together. Why couldn't she see that?

Chapter Seven

"That was quite a game. I had no idea the Quad City Thunders were so good." Jo's face still felt hot with excitement. "Did you see the way he waved at the crowd after he dunked that ball?"

"It wouldn't have been that close if they hadn't wasted the first half and had to play catch-up," Bill retorted, grinning. Kneeling before Rob's huge fireplace, he tried to coax a blaze out of a pile of kindling.

Rob glanced up as he opened a bottle of white zinfandel, and a beer for Jo. "All right, you two. Time to change the subject. Paula will be back in a minute, and she'll have our heads if we're still talking basketball."

Jo stood by the fireplace, letting the deep sense of contentment warm her like the heat from the fire. Yet her contentment was a sham, a fraud. *She* was a fraud. She stood there enjoying Rob's company, drinking his beer, soaking up the affection he offered, while the journals that could hurt him and shatter his family's reputation lay on her desk.

She had found a reason to avoid mentioning her discovery when he called Saturday. How could she tell him something like that long distance? That excuse had worked fine by phone, but what about Sunday night? He had gotten back early and taken her out to dinner, and still she hadn't said anything. Now it was Monday, and she couldn't find the words.

Jo frowned. She knew why she remained silent—she was afraid. Her news could spell the end for her and Rob, and she wasn't ready to face that. Not yet.

"Snack time!" Paula's cheerful voice cut off her gloomy thoughts. Rob's sister smiled as she shoved a serving cart loaded with popcorn, chips and dip, raw vegetables, and fat gulf shrimp through the doorway.

"Paula, you should have let me help," Jo protested. "I didn't know you were making a feast."

"All I had to do was pop the corn and open bags—Gretta did the rest before she left. Besides, you sports nuts needed a chance to rehash the game. Watching it once is enough for me."

Bill laughed and pulled his wife down onto the floor beside him. "I do like sports, but it's my only fault."

Paula grimaced. "The only one you admit to, you mean."

The men soon forgot their good intentions and went back to analyzing the game, but Jo searched for a topic that would interest Rob's elegant sister. What did you say to a woman who had everything? Fortunately Paula solved the problem for her.

"Rob tells me you're a writer. Sometimes I'd like to trade my job for something more glamorous, but I suppose even writing gets boring if you do it every day."

"There's a lot of truth to that," Jo said. "Where do you work?" She hadn't realized that Paula worked at all. She clearly didn't need to.

"Garfield School. I teach learning-disabled children."

Jo's eyebrows arched in surprise. She wouldn't have credited this petite, fashionable woman with the dedication necessary to teach school. But then, she wouldn't have expected Rob to put in the long, if irregular, hours he seemed to work. She was always misjudging people lately. Or maybe she always *had* thought in stereotypes and was just now realizing it. Could that be because of her feelings for Rob? She put the idea aside to think about later. "That must take a lot of patience."

"It does, but I love it. I'm crazy about kids." Paula's eyes darkened, but the look of haunted pain lasted only a moment before her cheerful mask dropped back into place. "So, what does a writer really do?"

"Sit in front of a computer until you think you're going to take root there." Jo chuckled. "I write mysteries and do some free-lance work. My latest project is a history of the Mississippi River Basin." Jo watched with amusement as the men wandered off to catch the highlights of the game on the late news. Rob had one thing in common with her brothers. They loved sports too.

"Sounds like an iffy way to make a living."

"It is, but I've always loved writing. I figured if I let myself get attached to a regular paycheck, I'd never take the risk."

A shadow crossed Paula's face again. Glancing toward the men to make sure they were still engrossed in the TV, she leaned forward and lowered her voice. "Yes, waiting too long doesn't pay. Bill and I put off starting our family, and now I can't seem to get pregnant. Maybe if I'd tried right away. . . ."

Jo's heart opened to the unhappy woman, and she reached out to pat Paula's hand. "Don't give up. These things take time. My mother tried for five years before Brian arrived; then the rest of us came as fast as she could deliver us."

Paula gave her a grateful look. "That's

encouraging. I'm going to have some tests done next week."

"Things will work out. You'll see." Jo hoped she was right. The misery in Paula's eyes tugged at her heart. Thank goodness she'd had the courage to do what she really wanted to do, to strike out on her own. . . . She glanced over at Rob and Bill, still hashing out the details of the game.

Yes, she was brave enough when it came to her job, but did her courage fail her when it came to men? It seemed to in Rob's case. Here she was, stuck on a fence post, afraid to give their relationship a real chance, just as afraid of saying something to destroy their new, fragile feelings for each other. She shook her head and turned her attention back to Paula.

"I hope you're right. I'd really like a baby." Paula shrugged, as if to chase off her distressing thoughts. "So you're writing a history. Has Rob let you look at the family records?"

"Yes, he has."

Paula nodded. "Ah, then that was the bait." Jo wondered what that meant, but Paula continued before she could ask. "I'm surprised Granddad agreed to let you into those trunks. He wouldn't even let us kids into the attic when I was growing up."

"I'm not sure Rob told him. Not everything in those records reflects well on the Porter family."

"Great." Paula rolled her eyes. "Granddad

is sensitive about his reputation. Rob isn't as bad, but he's still pretty stuffy about some things. What are you going to do?"

"I've tried to talk to Rob about it, but every time I mention my work, he changes the subject."

"That figures. He's probably afraid you'll go back to Oklahoma when you're finished with it." Paula smiled. "Well, I'm sure you'll think of something."

"I'd better." *And soon, before Joseph Porter hears about it.*

Jo frowned as she wondered why Rob made it so hard to talk to him. If Paula was right, he was stalling, trying to keep her around as long as possible. Jo hoped that was true. She'd thought he was just too wrapped up in his high-powered career to be interested in hers. But maybe she was making things harder than they should be, because she was afraid of losing him. No matter how many times she told herself that they had nothing in common, she missed Rob when he was gone.

She should have talked to him Sunday, because what she'd discovered Monday made doing so even harder. She had spent the morning at the newspaper morgue, and it was all bad news. The obituaries for July 12, 1898 had listed a Max Higgins, age thirty-four. Max had worked for Edward Porter for eight years. He died on July 9, the day Edward wrote that he'd "had to get rid of Max." Cause of death was listed as accidental drowning. Max left a wife and three children.

"Great game." Rob strolled away from the TV and dropped onto the sofa beside Jo. "Another beer?"

"Thanks, but I'm kind of tired."

He sighed. "I suppose you want me to take you home."

"That would help. It's a long walk." Jo smiled.

"And I suppose I don't get to see you until the weekend."

"I will be pretty busy," she said, trying to ignore the disappointment in his eyes. He didn't say anything as she said good-bye to Bill and Paula, who left at the same time, and the silence lengthened as he helped her into the car.

It was a long drive to LeClaire.

As if she didn't feel bad enough already, he cornered her when they got to her apartment. "Jo, we need to talk."

"Yes, we do," she said. Her voice was steady, but her heart beat wildly in her chest, and she felt a little dizzy. So this was it. How was she going to tell him? Just blurt it out and get it over with. "I've been meaning to tell you how my research has been going, and now's—"

"No, no, no!" He glared at her. "You're not going to put this off by talking about work! We need to talk about us, Jo. Every day I care more about you, but when I try to get closer, you back away. Yet you seem to miss me when I'm gone. You're driving me crazy. What's going on?"

"I . . . I'm just being cautious, Rob. You don't know me all that well and—"

"I know enough, Jo." He paced to her window and stared out at the dark river. "You're pretty and smart and kind, and we have fun together."

"How would you know what I'm like?" Her voice rose as her agitation grew. "We've known each other only a few weeks. For all you know, I could be an ax murderer!"

"Right!" He stalked back and glowered at her. "Just tell me this. What are you afraid of? Me or men in general?"

"I'm not afraid. I'm just being sensible!"

"Sensible? Hah! You're scared to death of me. Jo, I want to spend more time with you than just a few hours on weekends. I'm crazy about you."

She stared at him, shocked. He was right. She *was* afraid. Afraid of falling in love with him and losing him. Afraid of not measuring up, of his family's disapproval, and not just because of the things she had found in his family records. How could a simple country girl possibly please Rob's rich, powerful family?

"You're crazy, all right," she muttered, bitterness welling up inside her. "Crazy to think our relationship could go anywhere. We have nothing in common, Rob. Nothing."

He winced at her words, but he didn't give up. "That's garbage. We have our differences, but we respect each other. Please don't run away from me, Jo. I think I'm falling in love with you."

"You can't mean that," she gasped, stunned.

"I can and I do. Think about what I've said. I'll see you Saturday." With one last, searching look, he walked out of the apartment and down the dark stairs.

After he left, she went to bed, forcing her mind away from Rob's terrifying, tantalizing words. She finally drifted off to sleep, but her rest was disturbed by a steely-eyed old man who shook his finger in her face and thundered, "Stay away from my grandson!"

She was so tired Tuesday that she didn't get much done. Trying to straighten out the Porter mess and worrying about Rob had put her behind with her writing, and she wasn't catching up.

She was still dragging when she got to work at five P.M. The drive from LeClaire had been unusually tedious because of the fine, dry snow that had begun falling around noon.

At least the snow cut down on the number of gamblers. Tired as she was, it would have been hard to keep track of the usual ten to twelve players crowded around the table. What with the snow, the most she'd had to deal with was four, and she even had a few spells with nothing to do.

It was just after eight, three-fourths through the "dinner cruise," when she saw a familiar face heading for her table. Jo unobtrusively studied the man, but she couldn't place him. Where had she seen that sandy hair, those small green eyes before?

"Jo! How are you? I didn't know you worked here. This must be where I saw you before."

The man extended a perfectly manicured hand, and she shook it. The slight sneer in his voice jogged her memory. This was Rob's friend Jim—the one whose date had deserted him at the party. Jo didn't blame her. The guy had a real attitude problem.

"It's good to see you again," she lied, smiling her best meet-the-public smile. "Care to play a little twenty-one?"

"Sure." He pulled up a stool and placed a bet. Jo dealt the cards, face-up. At his request, she hit him with a five, which gave him twenty-two. Busted. Jo pressed her lips together. So Jim wasn't a cautious player. With a little luck, a person could play blackjack all night, as long as he followed the convention the house was required to use. Hit on sixteen, stay on seventeen. Then the odds were nearly even.

It was the wild players, the ones who trusted their "instincts" instead of the numbers, who lost big. They always thought they would win big too, but it rarely happened.

Jim was a talker. As he played, he kept asking prying, personal questions. Jo sidestepped most of them with only mild irritation, but she could tell from his sloppy mistakes that he was distracting himself. Or maybe he'd had too much to drink. Why did Rob hang around with such a loser?

She kept glancing around, hoping to catch another player's eye, but a table where one lone sucker kept losing wasn't very appealing.

Jo breathed a sigh of relief when he lost his

last chip. Under Iowa gaming regulations, all casino players had a two-hundred-dollar loss limit. She'd made a quick estimate of Jim's resources when he sat down. He'd started with nearly three hundred in chips, which meant that he'd either won earlier or found someone willing to bend the rules.

She grimaced. Where he'd gotten the chips wasn't her problem. She was just glad she had cleaned him out early. He looked like the type who would hang around after closing time and bother a woman.

"Better luck next time," she said with a wooden smile.

"Right," he said sullenly. His good mood had soured as his chips disappeared.

He was three steps away from the table when he turned back. "Say, if you get off soon, I'd be happy to buy you a drink."

Maintaining her smile was an effort. What kind of man would try to steal a friend's girl? "I'm afraid not. I work late tonight, but thanks, anyway."

"Oh. Maybe another time." Frowning, he stomped off.

Holly Sands paused at her table, balancing a tray of drinks. "What did you do to him?"

"Nothing much." Jo grinned. "Just cleaned out his wallet and blocked his pass."

Holly laughed. "That'll do it every time."

"Jim. What brings you by today?" Rob covered the papers he'd been studying and smiled. The man's huge ego often irritated Rob, but he hid his feelings behind a friendly mask. He'd grown up with Jim; they belonged to the same clubs. And Jim's family kept substantial accounts at the bank.

"I was in the area, so I just thought I'd stop by. Paula did a nice job on the dance."

"I'll tell her you said so. Last time I talked to her, she was still worrying because the decorations didn't match the table settings or something."

"I never noticed."

Rob rolled his eyes. "Neither did I, but you know how women are."

"I sure do. And speaking of women, I ran into that new girlfriend of yours yesterday." He lowered his voice to a conspiratorial whisper. "Boy, you really pulled one over on everyone!"

"I beg your pardon?" Rob arched an eyebrow and frowned. What could Jim be talking about?

"You know—when you introduced her as a writer. We all bought it—lock, stock, and barrel. Even I believed you!"

Rob laid down his pen and stared at Jim. "Why wouldn't you believe me? It's true."

Jim laughed. "Give me a break, Rob. We both know she's a blackjack dealer, a good one too. She cleaned me out last night."

"She's working on the boat as part of her research. Her latest project is a book on riverboat gambling," Rob explained uneasily. Why did he feel so uncomfortable talking to Jim about this? He wasn't ashamed of what Jo did. True, he wasn't thrilled knowing she was out alone late at night, but. . . .

"Right!" Jim guffawed. "That's a good one. I guess you'd better hope she doesn't decide to write a book about armed robbery or—"

"That's enough," Rob snapped. "Even if dealing cards was her only job, it's honest work. At least *she* works," he added pointedly.

Jim looked startled at Rob's words,

They even shocked Rob. He had never approved of the way Jim lived off his family's money, but he had always kept his opinions to himself. Until now. It felt great, saying what he really felt. He just hoped he hadn't cost the bank a customer.

"Now, if you'll excuse me, I'm behind on my paperwork." He forced himself to smile as he ushered Jim out, but he pretended not to hear Jim's nervous suggestion that they set up a racquetball date.

Rob gulped down half a cup of cold coffee and stared out the window. Why had Jim's visit upset him so? He'd always known the guy was a jerk. Unfortunately, he was a big-mouthed jerk. He would most likely repeat the things he had said to Rob to anyone who would listen, embellishing them as he went.

Jo was so proud, so fiercely independent. She didn't deserve that kind of treatment. Jim's cruel lies would hurt her, especially if she wasn't prepared. Even his own innocent offer to buy her a dress had offended her. He had realized that almost as soon as the words were out of his mouth. Rather than accept what she saw as charity, she had used her little windfall from the slots and taken an entire day off from her book to shop.

He smiled as he remembered how proud he'd been when he found out what she had done. He wished he could be that stubbornly independent. But he couldn't afford to be. He cared too much what people thought. In his job, he had to.

Jo cared what people thought too. She was just too proud to admit it, which meant she couldn't admit her hurt, either.

He couldn't shield her from hearing Jim's nasty insinuations, second- or thirdhand, but he could prepare her, perhaps lessen the damage. He'd better do it soon, though. Jim would waste no time telling everyone that the pretty Southern belle who had charmed them at the dance was really a blackjack dealer.

Chapter Eight

Rob fidgeted as Grace Van Hoosier poured brandy into a pair of crystal snifters. In the first place, he didn't like brandy, and in the second, the old lady had rattled on through a five-course meal about how she couldn't part with any of her beautiful antiques, *or* the land up in Wisconsin where she spent two weeks every summer, *or* the hot speedboat that hadn't been in the water since her husband died three years ago.

That was fine with Rob, except that she was getting low on cash, and as trustee of the trust her husband had left her, he had to sell something, whether she liked it or not. When he first suggested selling the land and the boat, she had become hysterical, so he had arranged to meet with her over dinner,

121

hoping to convince her that she didn't really need them.

He hadn't known she would be totally unreasonable. And he hadn't known he would be desperate to see Jo.

It was almost nine when he finally escaped. Rob growled under his breath. Jo must be on her way to work by now. That meant he'd have to wait until tomorrow to see her, or catch her when her shift was over. He turned his car toward LeClaire.

He parked in front of the decrepit bait shop near her house and looked up at her dark apartment. More than four hours to kill. He glared up and down the street.

Only a beer sign in the window identified the unpainted building as a bar. Rob wrinkled his nose as he walked in. The interior was dark and murky, the jukebox too loud, and the smell of stale grease and beer hung heavy in the air. He found a cracked, plastic booth near the back door and rested his head in his hands. It promised to be a long wait.

"What'll it be, mister?"

"How about a pitcher of beer?" he answered, taking in the exaggerated sway of the woman's hips as she moved away from the table. Dark-rooted, straw-blond hair, ragged at the ends, fell below her shoulders. Her lavender tank top was tucked into the waist of too-tight jeans. Tacky.

"Here you are." The woman set the beer on the table.

"Thanks." He handed her a five, but she lingered.

"I haven't seen you around. Are you new in town?"

As she smiled at him, it hit Rob that she might be offering more than a beer. He started to brush her off, but then he remembered the sneer in Jim's voice when he labeled Jo a blackjack dealer, as if that were something to be ashamed of. Jim's unfair judgment had hurt, yet he'd been about to judge this woman the same way. Who was he to condemn her? He had no idea what her life was like, who she was under the dangle earrings and garish makeup. She didn't interest him, but that was no reason to be unkind.

"Just waiting for my girlfriend." He made sure his smile was friendly.

"Oh." She looked a little disappointed, but then she brightened. "Does she live around here?"

"About a block away. She works on the *Iowa Lady*," he added.

"That must be great." She sighed wistfully. "I'd love to get a job on one of the boats."

Rob wasn't sure whether she was sincere or just making conversation, but he gave her the benefit of the doubt. "Have you filled out an application?"

She looked startled. "I never thought to do that. Do you think I'd have a chance?"

"I don't see why not. They always need

waitresses, and you're good at your job."

"Maybe I will. Well, I guess I'd better get to work."

Rob noted with surprise that she held her head a little higher as she walked off. It just proved that snap judgments about people could be all wrong. He wiped a spot off his glass and took a drink of cold beer.

By the time the bar closed, he was about to go crazy. Leaving a nice tip for the waitress, he stalked out of the bar. He climbed the stairway to Jo's door, but the apartment was still dark and silent. No wonder—it was a twenty-minute drive to LeClaire, and she probably had to close up after that last cruise.

What was he supposed to do until she arrived? Without really thinking, he turned the doorknob. The old lock rattled but didn't give.

Rob grinned and pulled out his wallet. This always worked in the movies. He picked out a gasoline credit card and slid it between the door and the frame, then blinked with amazement when the door came open. Stepping into the apartment, he shut the door behind him.

Jo hummed a little tune as she parked behind the building. It had been a good day. The table had been busy, but everyone had been in a good mood—good enough to tip well. She grimaced. From what she'd heard, Iowa gamblers were stingy tippers compared with their Las Vegas cousins.

Maybe she would use her tips for a new dress. Her usual wardrobe suited her fine most of the time, but it would be nice to have something pretty to wear for Rob.

She had her key in the lock and was turning it when she realized something was wrong. There was a light on in her apartment, and her key turned too easily. Her hand flew to her mouth. Someone had been in her apartment. What if he was still there?

Easing her key out of the lock, she backed toward the stairs. She was halfway to the sidewalk when the sound of her door opening froze her in place. Her heart pounded wildly, but her feet wouldn't move.

"Hey!" a male voice called.

"Keep away from me! I've got a gun," she lied. Finally her feet came to life and she started back down the stairs.

"Jo, what are you doing?"

She blinked. "Rob?" Relief coursed through her as she recognized his voice; then fury replaced it. He'd nearly scared her out of her wits. "What am *I* doing? What are *you* doing? I thought you were a burglar."

"You really should get a better lock," he said.

"I never had any problems with it until now," she snapped, stomping back up the stairs. "What do you want?"

"I talked to Jim today. It seems he ran into you down on the *Iowa Lady*."

"Yeah. So what?" Jo stalked past him and shrugged out of her coat. What did that have to do with his breaking into her apartment in the middle of the night?

"He seems to think we lied to him about what you do for a living."

"We?" Jo felt her temper fraying. First he'd nearly scared her to death; now he was upset because one of his precious friends had found out that she was a blackjack dealer. "I don't recall denying that I'm a dealer."

"Jo, will you calm down? I just wanted to let you know what he was saying. Chances are he's going to spread it all over town, and I wanted you to know. I ... didn't want you to hear it from someone else first."

"Hear what? That I work on a gambling boat?" She stared at him for a long minute, pain replacing her anger. So that was it—he was ashamed of what she did for a living, so he assumed she was too. He thought she wouldn't want word of her second job spread around town.

"I'll tell you something, Rob." Not looking at him, she tossed her coat onto the sofa. "I'm a blackjack dealer, just as much as I'm a writer. Since that bothers you so much, you'd better be getting back to your fancy house and your fancy friends."

"Jo, that's not what I—"

"Just go!" She stalked into her bedroom and slammed the door. Ear to the door, she waited until she heard the outer door close, then threw herself across her bed and cried herself to sleep.

"Jo, what's wrong? Your face is all puffy, and you look like you haven't slept in a week."

Jo grimaced at her reflection. "Last night wasn't one of my best nights," she admitted.

"What's wrong?" Holly turned her back and lifted her fluffy red hair off her neck.

"Man trouble, what else?" Shrugging, Jo zipped her friend's uniform.

Holly's eyes widened. "Did you have a fight with your new boyfriend?"

Jo applied cover stick to the deep circles under her eyes. She hoped she could get through her shift without crying. She hadn't cried yet, and she didn't plan to. "Yes. It was just awful."

"What happened?"

"First he broke into my apartment and nearly gave me a stroke; then he told me he was ashamed of me."

"But why would he be ashamed of you?"

"Because I'm a blackjack dealer!" She blinked furiously, but a tear escaped, anyway. "He thinks he's too good for someone like me!"

Holly's eyebrows drew together. "He said that? The rat!"

"He might as well have." It was no use. Tears spilled over, tracking mascara down her cheeks. Between sniffles she told Holly about her argument with Rob. "I don't know what he expects me to do!" she wailed. "Quit my job so he won't be embarrassed in front of his friends?"

"What a creep!" Holly said. "I'll tell you what I'd do. I'd change my locks and tell him to get lost."

"But I don't want him to get lost. I want him to understand!" She could feel Holly's concerned eyes on her, but she didn't manage to stop sobbing until Holly began dabbing at her eyes with a tissue.

"Come on, now stop that," Holly chided. "You look like a raccoon, and we're supposed to go on duty in five minutes. Tell you what. Some of the girls are going out for a drink after our shift. Why don't you join us?"

"I'll think about it." Jo smiled tremulously. "Thanks for listening."

By the end of her shift, she was feeling better, but she decided to pass on Holly's offer. After a sleepless night and two missed meals—she had been too upset to eat—she needed food and a warm bed, not alcohol.

"I'll walk you to your car, anyway," Holly said. After telling her friends that she would meet them at the lounge, she followed Jo into the parking lot.

Holly's eyes widened as they neared their cars. A red Mercedes had taken the space between Holly's car and Jo's old wagon, and a lone figure stood beside it, shoulders hunched against the wintry wind.

"Is that your boyfriend?"

"Sure is." Jo's heart lifted at the sight of Rob's broad shoulders.

"Nice car," Holly commented. "And it looks

like he brought you flowers. If I were you, I'd make him grovel a little before accepting his apology."

"Oh, I couldn't do that," Jo protested. "I just want to—"

"Well, I can!"

Before Jo could stop her, Holly stepped up to Rob and looked him over. "You're a jerk, you know that?" she said.

Rob's mouth dropped open as he stared at Holly.

"If I were Jo, I'd tell you where to get off. It's a good thing she's the forgiving type." She turned and flounced off to her car.

"That's my friend Holly Sands," Jo explained.

"I take it you told her about our argument." Rob still looked amazed.

"Obviously." Jo almost smiled. If her feelings weren't so bruised, his shock would have been comical. "What are you doing here?"

He thrust the bouquet he'd been clutching into her hands. "I came to apologize. Is there someplace we can talk?"

Apologize? She was tempted to throw herself into his arms, but she still hurt too much inside. Anyway, he was right. They did have to talk, but after last night she felt uneasy about inviting him to her apartment. "I haven't eaten since morning. Why don't we get some breakfast?"

"Fine. What's open at this hour?" Rob opened the car door for her, but she stood her ground.

"I'll take my own car. Otherwise you'll have to bring me back here." That way she could escape if he said anything else awful to her. "There's an all-night restaurant near here. Why don't you follow me?"

"All right." He didn't look pleased, but he nodded.

It was a short drive to the restaurant. The sign at the curb was a modern plastic affair, but old-fashioned neon still proclaimed, *Breakfast Served 24 Hrs.* across the building's face.

Jo picked up her flowers, so the cold couldn't wilt them, and led Rob toward the restaurant. Even at two in the morning the place was half full.

Rob smiled as he held the door for her. "I haven't been here since I was in my teens."

Jo studied the menu and finally ordered biscuits and gravy, fresh fruit, and milk. "They just don't make sausage gravy like they do back in Texas," she complained.

"This place used to make great cinnamon rolls, though," Rob said. "Do you want to try one?"

"I don't think so. I'll probably be full."

"You can have a bite of mine, then."

She watched his face and decided he was talking about food to put off discussing their argument. Why, he must be nervous! The idea charmed her, as did the fact that he looked as if he'd lost sleep too. He must have been as upset as she was.

She glanced at her flowers and smiled. They were ordinary daisies and carnations, wrapped in green paper that bore a local grocery store's logo. Knowing he'd stopped somewhere and picked them out himself made them more precious than long-stemmed roses. "Thanks for the flowers. They're lovely."

"I figured I'd better bring a peace offering after last night." He paused and sipped his coffee. "I'm sorry I broke into your apartment. It was a juvenile thing to do."

"I didn't mind your being there," she said, choosing her words with care. She needed to let him know how she felt without starting another fight. "It was just that you frightened me. A woman alone has to be careful."

"I understand completely." He nodded and looked relieved.

The waitress brought their food, and Jo took a bite of her biscuit. Any little greasy spoon in Texas could make better gravy, but she was hungry enough to eat an armadillo. She took another bite as she waited for Rob to continue.

"I've been thinking about the rest of our argument too," he finally said. "I don't think you understood what I was trying to tell you."

Jo looked up, startled. Could she have heard right? He blamed her for their argument? "I understood, all right," she said. "You're embarrassed because your friend found out that I'm a blackjack dealer."

"That's not true! In the first place, Jim's not a friend. He's just an acquaintance."

"Oh, that makes all the difference," she

drawled. "Does that make it all right that he tried to pick me up?"

Rob's eyes narrowed. "He did?"

She nodded. "Let me try a bite of your cinnamon roll." He could spare it. The roll covered the whole plate.

Rob frowned as he cut off a big hunk of pastry and transferred it to her plate. "No, it's not all right, but it does explain why he stopped by to give me a hard time. You hurt his pride when you turned him down."

"And he wanted to get even," Jo filled in. She noted that he didn't ask if she'd gone out with Jim. At least he trusted her that much, but she still didn't understand why he was so upset about what the man might say. Working at the tables wasn't something to be ashamed of. Rob must think it was, though. "What am I supposed to do? Quit my job to protect your reputation?"

"Of course not."

"Maybe I should wear a wig so no one will recognize me."

"Jo, will you stop and listen? I don't care about that. I came out last night because I was afraid someone would say something mean to you and hurt your feelings."

"So you thought you'd save some time and do it first." She frowned. Why couldn't he accept her for what she was?

"You know that isn't true," he said softly.

She was immediately sorry she'd said it. She knew he hadn't deliberately hurt her, but she still didn't know what *was* true. "Then, what *did* you think?" she asked.

"I figured if you knew what he was saying, you'd be in a better position to ignore it—or defend yourself."

"I see. So you were just warning me that Jim was likely to spread lies about me."

"That's right. There's no telling what he'll say. Jo, I feel terrible about this whole thing. It was my fault in the first place. If I'd mentioned that you work on the *Iowa Lady*, he wouldn't have had any way to give you a hard time."

"It's not your fault. Strangers don't want to hear a person's life story. Besides, it's no big deal. I can take a little gossip."

"I just don't want you hurt."

"Thinking you were ashamed of me hurt," she admitted, looking down.

"Ashamed of you? Never! I wish I were as independent as you." He took her hands. "Friends?"

Jo glanced at the flowers beside her plate and smiled. "Friends." She pulled her hands out of his and stared at her roll. Now was the time to tell him about her meeting with his grandfather. After he'd made the effort to straighten things out between them, she owed him that honesty. She took a deep breath. "Since we're baring our souls, there's something I need to tell you."

"Go ahead."

She had almost hoped he would put her off

again. It would be a shame if her news drove him off, after they had solved their other problem. "I think I may have done a bad thing." Before he could respond, before her courage could fail her, she rushed on. "Before I met you, I talked to your grandfather about the Porter family records. He said I couldn't use them." She flushed as she recalled the way he had ordered her out of his office.

Rob frowned at her, making her squirm with guilt. "Why didn't you tell me before?"

"I didn't know he was your grandfather that first day. You don't look anything like him, and I thought he was from Clinton. It never occurred to me that such a grouchy old man could be related to you."

"Granddad does have his moods," Rob agreed.

"I discovered he was your grandfather the first day I got into the trunks, when I went to clean up for dinner. His picture is in your hallway," she explained. "I tried to tell you then, but you didn't want to talk about work. After that, it got harder and harder to bring it up. I was afraid you would think I deliberately misled you, and—"

"I know you wouldn't do that." He reclaimed her hand. "Don't worry about it anymore. I'll handle my grandfather. If he didn't want anyone to see that stuff, he should have destroyed it or taken it with him when he moved."

"He may not want me to use it. Some of

the things I found have never been published before." Boy, was that an understatement! She knew she should tell him everything, but a restaurant was no place to discuss family skeletons.

"I'll tell you what. You finish going through the diaries, and I'll talk to my grandfather. Then we'll get together and decide what to do."

"But—"

"No buts about it. Everything will work out, you'll see. Right now we both need some sleep. Tomorrow is a workday." He signaled the waitress. "Can you bring our check? And we need another sweet roll to go."

Jo smiled sheepishly when he handed her the wrapped pastry. "You should take this. I ate a lot of yours."

"Just remember me when you eat it."

It was a clear, cold night, and the stars overhead glistened in the blackness. Rob caught her by the shoulders and pulled her into his arms as they stood between their cars.

He kissed her so long that her toes began to turn numb from cold, but the rest of her felt delightfully warm. Finally she pulled away with a shaky laugh. "You're going to get us arrested for loitering, Rob."

"Okay, okay." Chuckling, he let her go and opened her car door. "See you Saturday."

On the way home she glanced fondly at the sweet roll and flowers. Rob always seemed to know the right thing to do. Maybe that was why she liked him so much.

Liked him? Who was she kidding? She didn't like Rob; she loved him. She felt it deep inside when he kissed her, knew by the dull ache in her heart when they were apart.

But love didn't change things. No matter how she felt about him, he came from a different world, a world she wasn't sure she could ever share. The flowers were a perfect example of it. Rob was so slick, so smooth. He always knew just what to do, while she struggled with the social niceties that came so easily to him.

Even if she could learn to fit into his world, was it worth the strain, or would she lose too much of herself in the process? She shook her head in frustration. No matter how she tried to tell herself different, they were still sheep and goats, oil and water. And everyone knew that oil and water didn't mix.

Chapter Nine

It was almost dark when Jo walked into the diner down the street from her apartment, slid into a dingy booth, and ordered a burger, fries, and a Coke. It was just as well Rob hadn't asked to see her tonight. She needed to think, and that was impossible with him around.

They had spent Sunday afternoon sitting in front of the fireplace in Rob's living room, playing dominoes and eating popcorn. It had been a pleasant time, reminiscent of long winter evenings with her family in Texas. And Rob had talked about marriage.

Oh, he hadn't actually proposed. If he had, she probably would have run right out of there and not stopped until she got to Arkansas. Jo smiled as she picked up her

137

glass. He'd thought he was being slick, subtly working the subject into their conversation, but he was about as subtle as a rodeo clown.

"Have you ever thought of having kids, Jo? Do you like moving around all the time? What about marriage? Do you plan to get married someday?"

Then he'd asked the kicker. "What kind of man would you want to marry?"

She hadn't known how to answer that one. You didn't pick a husband the way you bought an automobile, comparing his features and drawbacks. Finally she had whispered, "I'd have to love him."

She'd been relieved that he didn't ask the next question. She couldn't lie to him, not about something so important, yet admitting that she loved him wouldn't do. One of them had to use their head instead of their heart, and it looked as if she was it. Rob had clearly lost his.

He hadn't quite said he loved her, but she could see it in his eyes. And she was tempted, so tempted.

What to do? She bit into her hamburger and chewed slowly. The idea of marrying Rob was appealing; she couldn't deny it. He was handsome and charming, kind and considerate—everything a woman could want in a man.

That was the problem. The very things that made him so appealing made their relationship impossible. He deserved a traditional woman, a woman who could be a foil to his high-power career. A bridge-party kind of woman, one who could flourish in his shadow.

Jo knew she could never be that kind of woman. She'd worked too hard developing her career to give it up, but she could hardly expect Rob to tell his friends that they couldn't make up a golf foursome because his wife had a deadline. Or postpone an important dinner party so she could run off to Round Lake, Minnesota, to research local Indian customs. There was no way they could meld their lives into a harmonious whole.

Besides, Rob didn't realize it yet, but his ancestor's diaries stood between them. Any way his talk with his grandfather went, there were going to be hard feelings. If she used the records, the elder Porter would never forgive her, and that would make a marriage difficult. How could Rob help holding it against her if she hurt his family?

Yet, if Rob told her she couldn't use the records, after he'd offered them to her, she would resent it.

She had tried to tell herself that they weren't important, but it simply wasn't true. In terms of local history, the diaries were a major find, and writing her history without them would be forfeiting the book's chance to make a real mark. They might even mean the difference between a popular book and one of only scholarly interest, because the public loved a scandal.

They weren't her records. If Rob said she couldn't use them, she couldn't. She'd tried to get around that conclusion in her mind, tell herself that Annabelle Martin's records said the same thing, but that argument wouldn't fly. She never would have discovered the Martin records if not for Rob's journals.

Lingering hard feelings were the best that could happen. The worst was that Rob might talk to his grandfather and never speak to her again.

It was ironic, really. The very thing that had brought them together would end by tearing them apart. She took a long, melancholy swallow of Coke.

"Hello, stranger," a familiar voice murmured, almost in her ear. Jo nearly knocked over her glass as she swiveled to stare into laughing brown eyes.

"What are you doing here?"

"Looking for you. I called you earlier, but you weren't home, so I decided to take a chance and drive out. When no one answered at your apartment, I scouted the parking lot and found your car."

"What did you do then? Start canvassing the area?" Jo grinned at a mental picture of Rob wandering around, looking for her.

"It wasn't much of a job. Anyway, I finished up early and thought I'd see if you wanted to get some dinner, but I'm obviously too late."

"Sit down and have a burger with me, anyway," she invited. "They're not bad."

The waitress appeared, and Rob gave her his order.

Over supper, they made small talk and held hands. The smile in Rob's eyes, the way he couldn't seem to get enough of her, made her feel so warm, so loved, that she wished the evening would never end.

She laughed about his latest battle with a spoiled young man who refused to understand why he couldn't get more money from the trust his aunt had left him, and then Rob surprised her by asking how her day had gone.

She remembered what his sister had said—that talking about her work probably scared him. After all, her job had brought her to Davenport, so it might someday take her away.

Tonight he didn't seem worried about that. Maybe he felt more sure of her after they had talked about marriage, even obliquely. Whatever the reason, she was relieved. It was hard to avoid talking about your work when you put as much time and love into it as she did.

This was the perfect time to tell him what she'd found in his family records. He was in the mood to listen, and he obviously hadn't talked to his grandfather yet, but she couldn't find the courage. Instead, she found herself describing the dresses she had discovered in a local accountant's basement. "Her great-grandmother was a singer. She saved every dress she wore onstage. We tried them all on and took pictures of each other for posterity. I'll show you when I get them developed."

"It must be exciting when you find something like that." Rob stuck a greasy French fry into his mouth and washed it down with beer.

"Oh, it is. I suspect it's the same feeling an archaeologist gets on a dig, minus the gritty fingernails." Jo smiled, but then she remembered how excited she'd been when she discovered that Rob's ancestor was a blackmailer. Her excitement had faded soon enough.

She finished the rest of her hamburger quickly. She just wasn't made for this kind of secrecy. Even losing Rob was better than feeling like a liar. "By the way, have you had a chance to talk to your grandfather?"

"Not yet. I didn't want to waste an evening I could spend with you, so I'm having dinner with him tomorrow. You are working Tuesday, aren't you?"

"Sure am." She frowned. Two days to wait. Or she could just tell him now and get it over with. She could feel his puzzled eyes on her.

"Don't look so worried, Jo. Everything will work out fine."

"I hope so," she said with a sigh. "I never wanted to cause you any trouble."

"Trouble?" He laughed softly. "You're no trouble, believe me. Now let me walk you home. And stop fretting about Granddad."

"But—"

"No buts about it. You Texans worry too much." He pulled her to her feet and silenced her protest with a kiss.

Jo let him lead her back to her apartment, but she couldn't stop worrying. She was disappointed when he didn't come in. His presence would have kept her gloomy thoughts at bay, but he was right. Tomorrow was a workday.

She kissed him good night, clinging tightly to his neck for a moment, trying to soak up his calm strength. Then she went inside and got ready for bed. Sleep didn't come easily, though, and even after she fell into a restless doze, her dreams were haunted by a deep sense of dread.

Rob grinned as he pulled away from the curb. It was about time things started going his way. He had begun to despair of convincing Jo that they were made for each other, but the last few days had proved him wrong.

Paula had apparently been right—Jo just needed time to get to know him, and those old trunks in the attic had given him the time he needed. Of course, there was still the problem of his grandfather to deal with, but he'd handle that tomorrow. Granddad might as well get used to Jo's snoopy ways, because if he had anything to say about it, she was going to be around for a long, long time.

He parked the Mercedes in the garage and went into the kitchen, looking for a snack. Greasy burgers just didn't qualify as supper, in his book. As he rummaged in the refrigerator, he paused to glance up at the clock. Nearly eleven. What time did that make it in Europe?

Rob tossed some sliced cheese and carrot sticks on a plate and poured himself a glass of milk. About five A.M., but he needed to call early if he wanted to catch his parents in their hotel room. Their itinerary was on the desk in his study, so he took his food in there to call. Settling into his roomy, leather desk chair, he dialed.

The phone in their motel room rang eight times before a groggy voice said, "Hello?"

"Mom?" Rob grinned. His mother was a sound sleeper. "It's Rob. How's Paris?"

That shook her out of her daze. "Rob? Robbie? Is something wrong? Your sister is okay, isn't she?"

"Don't panic, Mom. Everything is fine." He chuckled. His mother never had been one to stay calm in an emergency. "I just have some news for you and Dad. Is he awake?"

"I am now!" the elder Robert Porter's gruff voice came onto the line. "What is it? Is there a problem at the bank?"

"No, no. Nothing like that."

"Then why are you calling at this hour?" he asked.

"Are you sitting down?" Rob deliberately drew out the suspense, partly for the fun of it, partly because he wasn't sure how his parents would take his news.

"Of course I'm sitting down. I'm in bed!" the elder Porter shouted. "Now, what is it?"

"Dad, I'm thinking about getting married."

"Why don't you tell Frances instead of waking me up?"

Rob frowned. He'd forgotten that he hadn't told them he'd stopped seeing Frances. Maybe this phone call hadn't been such a good idea, but making it had been pure instinct. When a man decided to get married, he let his parents know first. And, if possible, got their blessing. That might not be possible in this case. Not when they still thought he was dating Frances.

"Didn't I tell you Frances and I aren't seeing each other anymore?"

"When did that happen?"

"Several weeks ago." Rob could hear his mother's voice in the background, demanding that his father share the phone. He spoke a little louder, so they could both listen, and wished he hadn't called. "The woman I want to marry is named Joanna Christenson, and she's a writer."

"That's not a familiar name. Is she from Davenport?" his mother asked.

"No, she's from Texas, Mom. She's here to write a book."

"A writer? That doesn't sound very stable." His father sounded doubtful or sleepy; Rob couldn't tell which.

"It isn't." Rob grinned, imagining his father's expression. "She's dirt poor and proud of it. Comes from a big family, and her father works in the oilfields down there."

"Look, Rob, I'm sure she's a very nice girl," his mother said, "but she hardly sounds like marriage material. What if she doesn't get along with your friends? I'm not sure a girl like that would be happy. . . ." Her voice trailed off.

He wondered if she knew how bigoted she sounded. Probably not. Much as he loved his mother, she tended to value people by the size of their cars and checking accounts, the prestige of their careers. Well, she'd just have to get over it or be miserable. He couldn't pick his wife to please his parents.

"If she doesn't like them, I'll have to find new friends," he said, just to bait her. "Maybe we'll move to Texas. . . ."

"Rob! This is no laughing matter. We're talking about your *life* here."

"That's right, Mom," he said softly. "It's *my* life we're talking about, and I want Jo to be a part of it. I'm going to propose to her the next time I see her. I was hoping you would give me your blessing."

"Are you sure you love her, Rob?" his father asked.

"I'm sure, Dad. When you meet her, you'll understand why."

"Then you have my blessing."

"Thanks, Dad." He thought he was going to have to do without his mother's approval, but then he heard his father growl, "Now, Sharon. . . ." He couldn't catch the rest, but after a moment she came on the line.

"Don't you dare get married before we get back! You've given me trouble since the day you were born, and you are not, I repeat *not*, gypping me out of a fancy wedding!"

"Don't worry, Mom. I'm not planning to elope."

Rob breathed a sigh of relief when they hung up. Two down, two to go. He really wasn't too concerned about his grandfather. The old man fussed and blustered, but he was a good old guy at heart. Jo was his main concern. She had seemed receptive to the idea of marriage, but to him?

There was only one way to find out. He would have to ask.

He headed out to his grandfather's condo right after work Tuesday. Joseph Porter met him at the door. "Rob! It's about time. I picked up some ribs on the way home from the Foundation."

"Hi, Granddad." Rob walked into the fashionably modern living room, sat down by the fireplace, and held his hands out to the heat of the gas log. The place always amazed him. How could anyone survive in a place like this, after living in the house on the hill? His grandfather didn't seem to mind, though. Rob knew for a fact that he'd picked out the hideous abstract painting over the mantel himself.

The old man set out the ribs and coleslaw and opened a bottle of good red wine. Rob smiled. None of this was on his grandfather's diet, but for once he didn't say anything. He had more important things to think about, and the old man was usually pretty good about eating what he should.

"So what's the problem?" Joseph Porter asked after they were seated.

"What makes you think there's a problem?"

"One, you haven't been over for weeks, and two, you aren't crabbing at me about the ribs."

"There's no problem, really. I do have some news, though. I've met the woman I intend to marry." *If she'll have me,* he added silently. "I'm going to pop the question in a day or two."

"About time." The old man bit into a rib, then wiped the barbecue sauce off his chin. "I was beginning to think you were going to stay a bachelor. Is it that Frances woman?"

"No."

"Good. I never did care for her."

Rob looked at his grandfather in surprise. He'd never had a clue that Granddad didn't like Frances.

"So what's her name? Do I know her?"

"Not really." Unless he counted the time he threw her out of his office. "Her name is

Joanna. Joanna Christenson."

His grandfather's gray eyebrows drew together. "Now, where have I heard that name before?"

"I think you met her once. She's a writer. She came to see you about some old family records."

"Her? You want to marry that busybody?"

"She's not a busybody, Granddad," Rob explained with as much patience as he could muster. "Research is her job."

"I don't call poking your nose in where it doesn't belong, prying into people's lives, much of a job." The elder Porter set his plate down and stalked over to the window. "How did she get her claws into you?"

"She didn't exactly get her claws into me," Rob said. "She rescued me from a snowstorm, and I tracked her down afterward and asked her to have dinner with me."

"A likely story." Joseph sniffed. "She was probably just looking for a way to get at you. And you fell for it—hook, line, and sinker."

Rob stood too. How could his grandfather talk that way about Jo? He didn't even know her. "I didn't fall for anything, Granddad. I'm in love with her."

"And I suppose you think she loves you." The old man's watery blue eyes flashed with unexpected life. "Don't you see, Rob? She's just using you to get to those records."

"I hardly think so, since I offered to let her use them a couple of weeks ago."

"*You what?*" His face turned so red that Rob rushed to his side, half afraid that he was having a stroke. "Are you out of your mind, boy? Those are our private family records. I never would have left them in the house if I thought you'd do a fool thing like that."

"Well, you did leave them, and I used my best judgment. It's too late now."

"Judgment—you call that judgment?" His silver hair bobbed as he paced the length of the living room. "You never did have any sense, but this tops it."

Rob wasn't sure whether to burst into laughter or make a run for the door. He'd never seen his grandfather so upset. And over a few old records! "What's the big deal?" he asked. "They're just a bunch of old diaries and account books. Don't you think you're overreacting?"

"Overreacting?" the old man asked incredulously. "Have you read those journals?"

"No, but—"

"Then you don't know what you're talking about. Do you remember hearing about Edward Porter?"

"Of course. The riverboat magnate. The man who built the Porter fortune."

"Right, except he didn't build it on profits from those riverboats. He was blackmailing half the politicians in Iowa!"

Blackmail? Rob sat down in the nearest chair because his knees didn't feel as if they would support him. "There must be some mistake."

"No mistake," the elder Porter said grimly. "Edward Porter was a criminal, pure and simple, a blackmailer and a murderer. It's a miracle he was never caught. He was over fifty when he finally gave it up, and by then there was plenty of money for his son, my father, to open the bank."

"I never knew," Rob said softly.

"No one did. And no one would have, if you hadn't let that snoopy writer read our records." His grandfather sat down with a sigh. "It's partly my fault, I suppose. I should have burned that stuff, but I just couldn't. Unpleasant as it is, it's who we are. Now I suppose everyone will know."

"Maybe you'd better tell me everything, Granddad. Then I'll see if I can straighten things out with Jo."

It was after eleven when Rob left his grandfather's condo. He drove slowly, letting habit take him home. His head was too full of what he'd heard to concentrate on the road.

When he pulled into the garage, he flipped on the light and stared at his beautiful red Mercedes. He'd bought the car with the income from a trust fund, one that had been set up years ago. The principal had come directly from Edward Porter, thanks to his good fortune in the riverboat business.

Good fortune, indeed. Rob snorted. It was strange to look at the car and realize that

it was bought with blood money. He wasn't
sure how he felt about that. It had happened
so long ago, there was an air of unreality to
the whole thing.

Of course, he wasn't pleased to find that
his ancestor hadn't been the white knight
he had imagined, but what did it have to do
with him, really? He was only responsible
for his own conduct, not his father's or his
grandfather's. Certainly not what a distant
relative did. So where was the shame?

Yet, it was there. He could feel it, like dis-
covering that the gravy stain didn't completely come out of your tie. First you're surprised,
then you wonder if everyone else can see it.

Yet, it was so long ago. Considering the
good the Porter family had done for Davenport since those days, he could hardly
believe that airing Edward Porter's mis-
deeds in some obscure history book would
destroy their reputation. Who read history
books, anyway?

His grandfather didn't see it that way, how-
ever. Before Rob had left, Joseph had handed
down one of his famous orders. "Get those
books back from that woman, Rob. And while
you're at it, make her promise not to use
what she's found. She could ruin us!" As Rob
had walked down the drive, the old man had
shouted after him, "And do it now!"

Rob hadn't reminded the old man that
he wanted to marry Jo—the timing hadn't
seemed right. Anyway, he had time. He

would have to clear this mess up once and
for all before he mentioned marriage, even
though waiting gave him a bad feeling in
his gut. As if she might slip away from him
again.

Why hadn't she told him what those records contained? If he'd known, he might have
been able to do more than gape stupidly when
his grandfather blew up. Maybe he could
have reasoned with him. As it was, there
was only one solution that would restore
family peace.

He would have to get Jo to promise that she
wouldn't use the records. But was that fair?
He'd told her she could use them. And there
was another problem. What if she refused to
forget about the information? It was spicy;
he'd admit that. The kind of thing some writ-
ers would do whatever they had to for, even
lie to the people who loved them.

Doubt.

It was a terrible thing. Once planted, those
seeds of doubt just wouldn't wither away and
die. They kept poking their ugly heads up,
making him worry and wonder.

As he let himself into the kitchen, he tried
to capture the happiness he'd felt before he
went to see his grandfather, but it was no use.
Hope and love couldn't grow with doubt.

And that meant there could be no marriage
proposal until he talked to Jo and wiped away
his doubts.

Chapter Ten

The lights flashed, the slot machines jingled their musical invitations, but there weren't many takers. That wasn't too surprising on a wintry Tuesday night. The tour-bus business slowed down when the warm weather disappeared, and those buses that still ran tended to arrive on the weekends, from nearby Chicago and St. Louis. And who among the locals could gamble until two A.M. and still get to work on time?

That was fine with Jo. The slower pace gave her time to people-watch, to enjoy the boat's rich, old-timey atmosphere. Tonight had been perfect. She'd had players at her table all night, but not so many that the game demanded her full attention.

Most people would come up to the table,

play a few hands, lose, and wander off to
find a game that suited them better, but
a few, the winners, would stick around. If
they didn't lose too often, they might stay for
the whole "cruise." When that happened, she
often heard their life stories as they played,
especially if the table was nearly empty.

Tonight her "regulars" were three older gentlemen from Waterloo, Iowa. One
had combed his few strands of hair over
his balding pate and sported a respectable
paunch; the other two had some serious
gray. Jo would have categorized them as
senior citizens, but they probably thought
of themselves as middle-aged, judging from
the cut of their suits. The ones who admitted their age usually dressed accordingly—in
easy-care polyester and comfortable, full-cut
shirts.

These guys thought they were slick too.
From the way they tossed gambling terms
around, she suspected they must be poker
buddies back in Waterloo. Maybe they'd come
to the Quad-Cities on business or to escape
from their wives for a few days. Either way,
they'd decided to try the casinos while they
were here.

It was probably their first time, even
though one of them mentioned Las Vegas
a couple of times, in that overly casual
voice people used when they wanted you
to notice. Jo wasn't fooled. A short course
on dealing cards and a few months at the

tables hadn't exactly turned her into a pro, but this guy was really green. You could tell by the way he watched his cards, glancing at them every few seconds as if they might change suits on him.

Jo smiled tolerantly. Let them have their little adventure. They weren't bad, as tourists went. They hadn't tried to pinch Holly when she brought them a round of drinks, or taken off their wedding rings before coming to the casino. A lot of men did that. Did they really think women didn't notice the bare, white spot where it belonged?

"So what about you, Jo?" the bald one asked, squinting at her name tag. "You don't sound like an Iowan."

"Actually, I'm from Texas. I came up here to work on the riverboats," Jo drawled. Explaining that she also considered herself an Oklahoman, or that she was writing a book, was too complicated. Besides, mentioning her writing was dangerous. When people heard that she was a writer, they often insisted on regaling her with long, boring stories that would be "perfect for her book."

"That's a big change." The one with the paunch studied the extra card she'd dealt him, then snorted in disgust. "Well, I'm busted. How do you like the Midwest?"

"Oh, I like it just fine. The people are friendlier than I'd expected." She raked in the cards, paid one player, and swept the other bets off the table.

Automatically, she dealt the next hand and kept up her end of their desultory conversation, but her mind wandered. She *did* like the Midwest...but well enough to spend the rest of her life here?

She glanced out the boat's velvet-draped window at the white-covered world beyond. Snow had begun to fall since she'd come aboard. Hardly more than a fall of moondust, it shimmered and danced under the parking lot's mercury-vapor lamps. Holly had told her that it sometimes snowed as late as April, burying the crocuses under a cold white blanket.

Then it would be spring, with its tulips and lilacs, its drenching rains and tornados. Jo smiled. At least the tornados would be familiar. Oklahoma and Texas had plenty of those.

Everything else was so different, even the people. She'd heard that people were the same everywhere, but she just couldn't see it. These Iowans were so staid, so set in their ways. And it wasn't just Rob.

All a person had to do was look at the houses, especially in the rural communities. From largest to smallest, they were neat and well kept, never flashy, but seldom really run-down. There were no abandoned farmsteads, as there were in Oklahoma. These people hoarded what they had, made it last and made it multiply.

Houses that had stood since the Civil War still sported claw-footed bathtubs and ancient commodes, some refinished, some so well cared for that their original white porcelain surfaces still gleamed. "If it ain't broke, don't fix it," could have been the state motto, to Jo's way of thinking.

It seemed so strange to her, so foreign to the life she'd known. Yet there was an appeal to it, something peaceful and seductive. What would it be like to have a place to roost, a little corner of the world that was hers alone? Someplace that would always be there, that wouldn't change?

A man who would always be there, safe and solid, to lean on in good times and bad. Rob would be that kind of man; she was sure of it. If he truly loved her, nothing would shake his faith in her; no emotional storm would drive him away.

But did he really love her, or was he just fascinated by their differences? How could she be sure? He'd almost proposed to Frances, a woman he didn't even seem to like.

But he didn't marry Frances. He'd backed out at the last minute, faced the fact that he didn't love her. Despite his exaggerated sense of family duty, he wouldn't marry someone he didn't love. Well, neither would she, but that was no problem. She loved Rob.

Maybe that was why he had stopped short of asking her to marry him. Maybe he wanted to make sure. Of course, if he was going to propose, he'd probably want to do it the old-fashioned way, anyway. A casual afternoon together wouldn't do—he would want candlelight and flowers and all the other trappings of romance. A smile came to her lips.

Or maybe he was just waiting to get the mess with his grandfather straightened out. Because she'd been so worried, he might be afraid to suggest marriage until he could assure her it was taken care of. At first she'd doubted that he could make things right, but he seemed so certain, she had finally believed he could do it.

Almost believed, anyway. She still felt a little uneasy when she thought about it, but at least she didn't panic. She'd even marked the spots in her book where she planned to use the journals, although she had held off on actually changing anything.

The tinkle of ice in glasses brought her back to the present. Jo smiled as Holly set down a fresh round of drinks and graciously accepted the gamblers' tips and compliments.

She studied the men's faces, tried to imagine Rob as he would be in his sixties. Taller than these men, with his hair a distinguished silver like the photographs she'd seen in his hall. He was a runner, so he probably wouldn't have a paunch, but his hand-tailored suits would fit him differently as he aged. Would she be there to watch him change, to change with him?

Jo didn't know, but looking at the old gentlemen from Waterloo, she suddenly realized that she wanted to be. She smiled again. If Rob asked her to marry him, she knew what her answer would be.

"Jo, I need to talk to you tonight."

"Tonight?" Jo blinked at the receiver. "But I have to work tonight."

"I know, but I really need to talk to you. It's still early. Can't you come by before your shift?"

"I suppose I could, but I was planning to do some research this afternoon. My editor wants to see a partial manuscript week after next, and I'm way behind schedule."

"Look, I'm not asking you to throw your schedule to the winds. I just need to talk to you. It's important." He sounded impatient.

"Couldn't we talk tomorrow over lunch?" Jo suggested. Cold prickles raced along her spine. Rob sounded so upset. What could be wrong? Surely it was nothing—another out-of-town business trip. It couldn't have anything to do with his family records. He'd promised he would straighten everything out, yet he sounded almost angry.

There was a long pause. When Rob finally spoke, his voice was slow and measured, as if he were keeping tight rein on his temper. "Tomorrow is too late. Your research will be waiting for you tomorrow, just as well as today."

"Couldn't we discuss whatever's on your mind now, on the phone?" She knew before she asked

that she was wasting her breath. Rob was sometimes a bit pushy, but she had never before heard
such determination in his voice. It wouldn't hurt
her to rearrange her schedule this once.

"No. I have to see you. Can you come by the
house on your way to work?" he repeated.

"I suppose so," she answered doubtfully. "What
time?"

"As soon as possible. I can be there in half an
hour." The harsh note in his voice didn't invite
further negotiation.

"All right. I'll be there as soon as I can get my
things ready for work."

"Good. I'll see you then." He hung up without
saying good-bye.

He was leaving work early to meet her and
hadn't even invited her to dinner, Jo mused as
she threw her costume into her bag. Her sense
of trouble brewing sharpened.

On impulse she picked up the few Porter
diaries that she hadn't already returned. If he
wanted them back, she would be ready. And if
not, she might as well return them. They hadn't
provided any additional information. Marie Porter had been a shallow, grasping woman, and
probably not too smart. She'd never given a hint
that she knew about her husband's illegal activ-
ities, and her life had seemed to center around
the luxuries her husband's money could buy.

Jo wondered briefly if his wife's greed had
driven Edward to blackmail, then dismissed the
idea. He was a grown man, responsible for his
own actions. If he had taken to crime to satisfy

his pretty wife's longing for fine things, that was his fault, not hers.

She put on her coat and headed for the car.

By the time she got to Rob's house, she was a nervous wreck. She picked up the diaries and walked up to the big door. A woman Jo presumed was Rob's housekeeper answered the first ring. The stout, middle-aged woman studied her, as if wondering why she was meeting Rob in the middle of the afternoon. Or maybe Jo was just paranoid. Did servants care what their employers did? She hadn't a clue.

Gretta opened the door and motioned for her to come inside. "Good afternoon, Miss Christenson. He's waiting for you in his study. Will you be staying for dinner?"

"I don't think so. I have to be at work in a couple of hours."

"Maybe another time, then. Follow me." The woman led her down a long hallway Jo hadn't explored before. At the end, she knocked twice on a heavy wooden door and pushed it open. "Joanna Christenson is here to see you."

"Thanks, Gretta," Rob's voice rumbled. Jo could hear footsteps approaching; then he swung the door wide and motioned to her. "Come on in, Jo."

His gray three-piece suit was neat, as usual, but his dark hair was rumpled, as if he'd been running his hands through it. Dark circles shadowed his eyes, and his lips were set into a hard line. He looked like he hadn't slept last night.

"Well, here I am." Jo smiled tentatively. "What did you need to talk about that wouldn't wait?"

He didn't return her smile. Instead, he folded his arms across his chest and looked at her, his eyes dark. "I think you know."

Jo swallowed. Whatever it was, it must be serious. Why else had he called her here to this dark, gloomy room? Gretta had called the place a study, but it seemed more like a dungeon. Dark-wood bookcases lined two walls, and a massive desk and library table took up most of the available floor space. The chairs filled the room with the scent of leather, and brown-velvet drapes shut out most of the winter-gray light. Brass lamps provided uncertain illumination.

It was the kind of room she might have pictured his grandfather in. She couldn't have imagined Rob in such a room, but now, scowling down at her, he seemed right at home. Like an inquisitor waiting for his victim. But what had she done to deserve his scowl? She'd already made her confession about the records, and he had taken it well. Of course, she hadn't mentioned what they contained.

"Know? I'm sorry, Rob. I don't have a clue." She watched him nervously, clutching the journals to her chest.

"You don't?" His frown deepened. "Why didn't you tell me what was in those?" He pointed at the books.

"Why should I tell you? It's your family." She gripped the books a little tighter, as if they could shield her from his anger.

"Right." He laughed harshly. "And it seems my family has plenty of skeletons in its closet. I repeat, Jo, why didn't you tell me?"

"I . . . I thought you knew. After all, they're your relatives." That was only half true. Oh, at first she'd assumed he knew what he was doing, but once she understood the kind of person Edward Porter had been, she had doubted it. And she'd been pretty sure Rob's granddad would have a fit when he heard what his grandson had done.

"Right. That's why you waited so long to tell me that you'd already talked to my grandfather."

"I explained all about that," she said, sudden desperation making her voice come out high and tight. He seemed so cold, so distant, as if nothing she said could reach him. It was like a scene out of a nightmare. "You said you understood."

"I thought I did, but now I'm not so sure. Why didn't you say something about my ancestor's proclivity for blackmail?"

"I didn't want to upset you," she said, biting her lip to stop its trembling.

"Upset me?" His voice rose. "Upset me? Did you think I'd be less upset if I found out when I read your book? Jo, I'm *named* after that man. Robert Edward Porter! Did you ever think of that? Or didn't you care?"

"Why are you shouting at me?" Jo yelled, stung by his accusation. How could he accuse her of not caring? She'd lain awake more nights than she could count, worrying about how he would take it, what she should do.

"It's not my fault that your whole family is full of jerks!"

"Jerks? At least I'm not a sneak."

"I'm no sneak! I tried to tell you, but you were too self-satisfied to listen." A small part of Jo's mind told her that shouting never accomplished anything, but she ignored it. Her emotions drowned out her common sense.

"Maybe I would have listened if you weren't so afraid of commitment. Every time you mentioned your work, I'd start thinking you were about to head off to Timbuktu or something for your next project."

"I'm not afraid of commitment! And even if I am, I have a good reason."

"Oh, yeah? And what might that be?" He glared down at her.

"Maybe I'm not sure I want to commit to a . . . a snob!"

"A snob? Is that what you think of me?" He stalked over to the window. "You should take a good look at yourself. You wear your self-imposed poverty like a badge of honor and sneer at anyone who doesn't live hand to mouth." He shook his head. "I can't believe I'm standing here listening to this. You're a fraud, you know that? You accept the benefits of my money, then abuse me for having it."

Jo's stomach tightened and she had to blink fast to hold back the tears. How could he say that? After she'd been so careful to keep things fair, not to end up in his debt. She glanced down at the books in her hand. Maybe shallow and petty ran in the family. "Don't worry. I won't inflict my opinions on you anymore," she said tightly.

She considered throwing the diaries at him but couldn't quite bring herself to do it. Good or bad, they were history. She slammed them down on the desk and headed for the door.

Rob grabbed her arm and spun her around to face him. "Not so fast," he ground out.

"Take your hands off me!"

His eyes narrowed, but he didn't let her go. "We're not finished here. What are you going to do with what you learned?"

"That's all you care about?" she gasped. A tear spilled over, blurring her vision. "Your stupid family pride? I thought I meant something to you."

"Don't confuse the issue, Jo. We're talking about those records, not our relationship. This isn't just between you and me. It affects my whole family."

"You should have thought about that when you blithely handed over their secrets," she snapped. She jerked away from him, but he was too strong. She was trapped until he let her go.

"I didn't know what was in them."

"Neither did I, but you act as if this is all my fault."

Rob ignored that. "Promise me you won't use anything you found in those journals."

"And if I don't?" Jo's breath came in harsh, painful gasps, and she could feel the tears streaming down her cheeks. Her eyes burned, but they didn't hurt half as much as her heart. And she'd thought he loved her.

"I can't be responsible for what happens. There are laws about invasion of privacy, you know."

Jo glared at him through her tears. So that was the bottom line. If she didn't do what he wanted, he'd see her in court. She supposed she should feel lucky. Poor Max had crossed his namesake a century ago and ended up in the river.

"Since you don't trust me, I don't see what good my promise is. Do what you have to do, Rob, and so will I." She jerked away again, and this time he let her go. She turned and ran from the room, but the look of agonized shock on his face followed her, even after she slammed the door behind her.

She dimly registered the housekeeper's concerned face as she dashed out the front door, but she couldn't even mumble good-bye. Just putting one foot in front of the other and gulping in huge lungfuls of air was all she could manage.

It took three tries to get the key into the old station wagon's ignition; then she almost flooded the motor in her haste. She drove two blocks, half blinded by tears, pulled over to the curb, laid her head on the steering wheel and cried.

How could their conversation have gone so wrong? She couldn't even remember half of what they had said, but his words had hurt her. And from the way Rob had looked at her, she'd hurt him too.

And for what? A few old records. Records she couldn't use without Rob's permission, anyway. Whatever had possessed her to let him think she might? Because he'd struck her pride such a blow. First he had called her a snob; then he'd let her know that he didn't trust her. She had been so shocked, so hurt that she'd struck back any way she could.

And she had thrown away her chance of happiness.

Finally she dried her eyes and put the car into gear. A sense of wrongness almost overwhelmed her as she drove away from the big brick house on the hill, but right or wrong it was too late. Now she would never call it home, never wait eagerly there for Rob to arrive. And the worst of it was that he was partly right. She was just as responsible for this mess as he was.

Chapter Eleven

"That's just not right." Jo glared at the framed prints of the Mississippi that she had always loved so much. They didn't look right hanging over the sleek, black-vinyl sofa that had come with her new apartment. Or maybe it was her view of the river that was missing. If Dubuque, Iowa, had any riverfront apartments, she couldn't find them.

She'd had to settle for this modern monstrosity. Oh, it had all the high-tech appliances that her old place had lacked, but there was no charm to it. The price tag was nearly twice what she had been paying in LeClaire too, which meant she would have to work more hours to make ends meet.

That was too bad, because she didn't like

169

her new job. A call from her old boss had secured her a place on Dubuque's gambling boat, but there were no dealer jobs open, so Jo had accepted a cocktail-waitress position on the promise that she'd get the next available job at the tables.

Waitressing was worse than she had imagined. She had to wear gold leotards, decorated to look like Old West saloon-girl dresses, with a fluffy little black skirt that was an invitation to the male passengers. One of the other waitresses had shown her how to avoid overeager hands, but she still hated the job.

Maybe Holly had been right. Her last night on the boat, she'd let her friends take her out for a farewell party after her shift ended. They had gone to an all-night restaurant and ordered pie and ice cream. It had all been very pleasant at first, but then Holly had said, "I can't believe you're letting a man run you off."

Jo had scowled and denied it. "Rob really isn't the reason I'm leaving. My research here is finished, and it's time to move on."

"Right," Chris, a pretty brunette Jo didn't know well, said. "That's why you have such a long face. This guy must be pretty special, to upset you so much."

Special. She'd thought so, but she had been wrong. He was just another rich, spoiled man, more concerned with appearances than people. To her chagrin, she had started crying, right in the middle of the restaurant.

Holly had come to her rescue with a tissue and a pat on the shoulder. "He was a jerk, Chris. He let Jo think he loved her, but all he really cares about is his family and his reputation."

"That's not fair, Holly," Jo protested through her tears, even though she'd just thought the same thing. She couldn't stand to hear someone else say it. "It was partly my fault. I knew from the beginning that we were too different, but I ignored my common sense."

"You're different, all right. *You* care about your friends."

"It's not all his fault. I shouldn't have kept things from him."

"Well," Chris said, "if you feel that way, maybe the two of you should give it another try. Then you could stay here in Davenport. We were just getting to know each other."

"You could be giving up too easily, Jo," Holly added. "The one time I saw you two together, you seemed so right for each other. And the way he looked at you, I'd have sworn he was in love with you."

Jo had felt a sudden surge of hope. Could Holly be right? Did Rob love her? Then the hope faded. She had waited a few days before giving her notice, hoping he would call; then she'd had to stay another week while they found someone to take her place. In those two weeks she hadn't heard from him. If he cared, he would have given her some sign.

"I guess we were both mistaken, Holly," Jo had said with a sigh. Then she'd made herself smile and changed the subject to Holly's latest boyfriend. Soon everyone was laughing again. Jo laughed too, ignoring the stabbing pain in her heart.

It had taken three more days to locate an apartment in Dubuque and move, and still no message had come. The first few days in her new home, she had checked her answering machine anxiously, but it hadn't blinked once. Finally she'd shut the machine off. Coming home to no message was worse than not knowing if Rob had tried to call.

It served her right, in a way. She'd known from the beginning that sheep and goats don't mix. If she had listened to her common sense instead of her heart, she wouldn't be hurting now.

And for what? A juicy bit of scandal that she couldn't use. Despite the angry words she and Rob had exchanged, there was no way she could use those diaries without permission from their rightful owner.

She would have told him that, if he hadn't made all those accusations. Yet, it was just as well he had. What if she hadn't found out what he really thought of her? She might have married him, trusted his love. And the pain she felt now would be nothing compared to what she would have felt if she'd let herself love him completely, only to discover that he didn't trust her.

The best thing to do was to finish the book and get on with her life. Not that she would ever forget him. How could you forget someone who still held a piece of your heart?

She gathered up her notes on the Porter family and stuffed them into a big manila envelope. Then she penned a brief, impersonal note, assuring Rob that his family secrets were safe, and sealed the package. She dropped it into the corner mailbox as she left for work, but then she paused and stared at the box for a long minute. If only she could package up all the misery he'd brought her and mail it off too. Sighing, she headed for her car.

For Rent. Rob stared at the sign on the door that led to Jo's apartment in disbelief. He'd been gone only three weeks. How could her apartment be for rent?

He took the stairs two at a time, but the apartment was dark and silent. A shiny new lock on the door proved that Jo no longer lived there. She was too trusting to bother with fancy locks.

As he drove back to Davenport, he kicked himself for three kinds of fool. Why hadn't he tried harder to reach her? St. Petersburg, Russia, wasn't the end of the world, although it had seemed like it when he tried to place a call to LeClaire, Iowa. He had tried to call several times, after the first tense days when he and Paula had barely left the intensive-care unit's waiting room.

He should have let her know he was going, but his dad's call, saying that his mother had collapsed during their tour of The Hermitage and might not survive, had driven everything except calling Paula and getting plane tickets right out of his head. He had been halfway to Russia when he realized that he hadn't told Jo he was going.

By the time he and Paula got to St. Petersburg, he doctors were preparing to perform open-heart surgery, so he'd put off his phone call, just until his mother was out of danger.

When he finally dared leave long enough to find a telephone, he had run into one obstacle after another. First the transatlantic circuits were busy; then he got an operator who couldn't speak enough English to put his call through.

Day after day it had gone like that, and the few times he did get through, Jo's machine had answered. Rob growled as he pulled into his driveway. He should have gone ahead and left a message, but after their fight, he hadn't known what to say to a soulless machine.

He had jotted her a short, romantic note, full of apology and words of love, but maybe she never got it. If the Russians couldn't make their phone system work, was their mail service any better?

Maybe Jo had left a message on his machine. He hadn't bothered to check when he got home, just tossed his bags in the front hall and taken off for LeClaire.

There were messages on his machine, all right. Half a dozen from clients who couldn't function without him, a couple of racquetball invitations, and three insurance salesmen, but nothing from Jo.

There was a big stack of mail too. He pulled up a chair and sorted through it, looking for anything in a feminine hand. He almost tossed the big brown envelope aside, but something about the handwriting on the front caught his eye. He ripped the envelope open, and Jo's notes spilled out.

These are all my notes about Edward Porter. You should know I would never do anything to hurt you.

Jo

But *he* had hurt *her.* Without meaning to, without wanting to, he'd broken her heart and his as well. But why? Why did it have to be like this? They were perfect for each other. If only she could have seen past the superficial differences in their backgrounds, seen to the depth of his love for her! So they had argued. Most couples argued, and over more serious issues than a bunch of old records. They could have worked it out, if she hadn't been convinced that they were all wrong for each other.

If he'd had time, he could have proved he was the man for her, but now it was too late. Or was it?

Rob took another look at the envelope in his hands and smiled. The postmark was Dubuque, and a return address was printed neatly in the upper left-hand corner. Trust a writer to put a return address on all her mail.

He glanced at his wristwatch. Six o'clock, and Dubuque was two hours upriver. That wouldn't be a problem if he'd been sleeping regularly, but between his mother's sudden illness, jet lag, and his problems with Jo, it seemed like a year since he'd had a decent night's sleep. That was just too bad, though. He'd waited far too long to make things right, and there was no way he could wait another day.

He drank some milk straight out of the carton, grabbed the sandwich Gretta had left for him, and hurried out the kitchen door.

Jo was too tired to notice the frigid wind as she hurried up the dark stairs. She would have thought an expensive place like this could afford a decent hall light. The stairs were worse than her place in LeClaire.

She had her key in the lock when she noticed the light seeping out from under her apartment door. Strange. She could have sworn she'd left the place dark.

Cautiously, she unlocked the door and opened it a crack. Nothing seemed to be amiss, so she slipped into the room, leaving the door open in case she needed to make a quick escape. A glance told her that the living room was empty, so she eased across the rug and checked the bedroom. That was empty too. She walked back into the living room and shook her head. She must have been mistaken about the light. She had her hand on the outside door, ready to close it, when she heard the refrigerator door swing shut with a soft thud.

Her first instinct was to run, but something stopped her. What kind of burglar raided his victim's refrigerator? She tried to ignore the sudden pounding of her heart as she tiptoed to the kitchen door and peeked around the doorframe.

She didn't know whether to laugh or cry at the sight that greeted her. Rob stood in the middle of her kitchen, making a sandwich as if nothing were wrong. As if three weeks hadn't passed without a word from him. As if he had every right to be there!

Jamming her hands onto her hips, she stepped into the room. "How did you break into my apartment this time?"

Rob didn't even look guilty. He glanced up from the jar of mayonnaise and smiled at her. "I didn't. Your landlord let me in, right after I explained that I'm your brother."

"I can't believe he bought that!" Jo walked into the kitchen and plopped down on a stool, still trying to take it in. She'd thought she would never see Rob again, yet here he was in her kitchen, acting as if nothing had happened.

"Sure he did. I have an honest face. Besides, I bribed him." Rob grinned at her, but then his smile faded. "Seriously, I was going to wait downstairs, but it was cold. Here, I made you something to eat." He put the halves of the sandwich together and held it out to her.

Jo ignored the sandwich. If he thought he was going to walk back into her life without so much as an explanation, he could think again! "This is incredible. Not a word from you in three weeks, and now you waltz in here and offer me a midnight snack. What am I supposed to do, welcome you with open arms?"

"I would have called sooner, but I've been out of town."

"Right." Jo jumped up and paced to the window. "I suppose they don't have phones where you were."

"I couldn't seem to make them work. St. Petersburg is a long way from Iowa, Jo."

"St. Petersburg?" Jo turned to face him, startled. "Russia?"

"That's right. Mom had a heart attack and had to have emergency surgery. Paula and I flew over to be with her because they thought she might not survive."

Jo pressed her eyes shut to control the room's sudden whirling. She'd pictured him off with his fancy friends, playing racquetball and discussing the stock market, while he had been sitting in a drab hospital waiting room, praying for his mother's life. She opened her eyes and met his, and realized that his chin was shadowed with a day's growth of beard, his eyes red-rimmed.

"Oh, Rob, I'm so sorry! Is she going to be okay?"

He nodded, smiling faintly. "They say she'll be as good as new. Paula and Dad are still with her, and she'll be able to fly home in a couple of weeks. Of course, she's going to have to change her life-style. No more fatty foods, cut down the salt, plenty of exercise. . . . She's going to be impossible to live with for a while. Anyway, I tried to call you, but the few times I got through, your answering machine picked up. It's kind of hard to say 'I'm sorry' to a machine."

"You are? Sorry?" she asked, half hopeful, completely confused.

"Of course. I acted like a jerk, and we both know it. If I had tried to talk to you calmly instead of flying off the handle and making all those accusations, none of this would have happened. The fact is, I was still in shock from hearing all about Edward's bad habits."

"You called me a snob and threatened to sue me," Jo pointed out.

"You should know I didn't mean it. You didn't mean everything you said, either." He paused and studied her face, concern darkening his eyes. "Did you?"

The forlorn question tugged at her heart. "Of course not. I was already feeling guilty because I hadn't found a way to tell you what was in those records, and. . . ." She looked away because she found she couldn't say the rest with him searching her eyes. "And I was worried about where our relationship was going, so I overreacted. Those records were awfully tempting, but there's no way I could use them without your grandfather's permission. I will admit I spent a few hours trying to think of a way, though."

He took a step toward her, but he didn't try to touch her. "I know you well enough to know you wouldn't do anything to hurt *anyone,* especially not someone you care about. Anyway, while I was in Russia, I had a lot of time to think. There wasn't much else to do besides worry. There are a couple of ways we can handle those records."

"Such as?"

"I talked to Dad about the journals. He wasn't pleased to find out that his great-grandfather, Edward, was a class-A scoundrel, but it was a long time ago. His view is that we should be judged by what we are now, not what our ancestors were, so he doesn't care whether or not Edward's secrets become public. That means one possibility is to wait until Granddad is no longer around."

Jo felt the tight knot in her stomach unwind a bit. If Rob's father really believed that, maybe he wouldn't hold her unremarkable background against her. But it didn't solve the immediate problem. She still had a deadline to meet. She shook her head. "Sorry, but that won't work. My editor won't wait that long for the book."

Rob nodded. "I thought that might be the case, so I came up with Plan B. Maybe you could leave the juicy stuff out of the history book and use it as the basis for some kind of historical novel? You know, one of those speculative books where no one is quite sure how much is historical fact and how much is wishful thinking?"

"I don't know. . . ." Jo's voice trailed off as she considered the idea. It was intriguing— take a set of real events and fictionalize them. How much fact would she use and how much fiction? Almost before she knew it, she was sorting through information in her mind, deciding which tidbits to keep, which to ignore. Yes, it would be fun! She might even write a happy ending for Rachel Martin.

"Why not?" she asked, nodding. "I'm sure I can do it, and no one would know for certain what is truth and what's fiction."

"Great." Rob didn't smile as he set her sandwich on the spotless white kitchen table. "Now that we have that solved, I think it's time to talk about you and me."

Jo swallowed and forced herself to meet his eyes. "I know."

"It's pretty simple, really," he said, moving close enough to close his big hands over her shoulders. "I love you, and I think you love me. We should get married."

"If only it were that simple, Rob." She took a shaky breath and wished she could bury her face against his chest, forget the words she had to say. But she couldn't. She had to be sure he understood what they were up against. If he did, he might not want her.

She swallowed her fear and continued. "Marriage is more than that rosy glow we feel when we're together. It's common goals, shared interests and values. Without that, the glow will fade fast, leaving nothing but hard, cold duty to keep the marriage going."

"So?"

Jo frowned up at him, exasperated. Why did he have to make everything so difficult? "So," she said carefully, "we have a problem. We don't have any of those things, Rob. We come from different worlds. I doubt that you can even imagine what my life was like back in Texas. I know I can't understand what it must have been like to grow up a banker's son."

"I'll agree we have different backgrounds, but—"

She shook her head. "It's not just different backgrounds, Rob. *We* are different. We don't think alike. The two of us married would be like pasturing sheep and goats together. I'm just not sure it would work."

He looked so fierce that for a moment she thought he might shake her, but instead, he pulled out a kitchen chair and sat down, taking her with him. She would have wriggled out of his arms if it hadn't felt so good to let him hold her. A small, involuntary sigh escaped her.

"For a smart woman, you can be awfully stupid sometimes," he said. "Why would you want to marry someone who is just like you?

A man and a woman should complement each other, one's strengths making up for the other's weaknesses. Besides, we're not as different as you think." His arm tightened around her shoulders, pulling her against his chest. "We have all kinds of common interests— reading, sports, Chinese food. . . ."

Jo laughed softly. "That's hardly enough reason to marry."

"Neither of us likes parties, and we enjoy travel."

"True, but how would you feel when I went off to research a book while you had to stay here and work?"

"I'd be just fine, as long as I knew you were coming back. You survive my business trips, don't you?"

"I hadn't thought of it that way," Jo admitted.

"Even more important," Rob continued, "our values are similar. We both care about the people around us and believe in honesty and consideration for others."

"And neither of us manages to live up to those ideals all the time," she said, smiling tremulously.

"That's right, Jo. We're real human beings, with real faults." He cupped her chin in his hand and turned her face up to his. "We have one other thing in common," he murmured. "We love each other. With a little tolerance, that will make up for our differences."

Jo looked into his eyes and realized that

he was right. Love was what counted, and there was no mistaking the love in Rob's eyes. Biting her lip to still its trembling, she nodded. "I do love you, Rob."

She felt the breath whoosh out of him in a huge sigh, and she smiled. So he hadn't been as sure of her love as he'd made out. She rested her head against his chest and reveled in the feel of his arms closing around her, cradling her against him. Reaching up, she wrapped her arms around his neck and pressed her lips to his in a long, sweet kiss.

When they finally came up for air, Rob smiled down at her. "I guess it's settled, then. We'll start planning the wedding as soon as Mom and Dad get back from Russia. When the doctor releases her, we'll get the guest list together, and maybe fly your mother up here to help plan things."

Jo looked at him in surprise. One minute he'd been trying, ever so sweetly, to convince her that they should *get* married; now he was issuing orders like a drill sergeant.

"Not so fast," she drawled. "There are still a few little details to be settled."

"Such as?"

"Kids, for instance. With a great big house like that, I think we should have at least three or four."

Rob gulped, but then he nodded. "Three, anyway. We can talk about number four when the time comes."

"And we'll need a dog and a couple of cats."

"No problem."

Jo hid a smile. He'd taken that better than the idea of a big family. She decided to push a bit more, just for the fun of it. "And a parakeet. We'll definitely need a parakeet."

Rob frowned. "No birds. I'm a reasonable man, but please, Jo, no birds!"

She couldn't help it. She burst out laughing.

He stared at her for a long moment; then he laughed too and ruffled her hair affectionately. "I was being pushy again, wasn't I? Telling you how we're going to handle the wedding instead of discussing it with you."

"Just a bit," she said, snuggling closer, "but I know how to deal with pushy men. I just love them until they give it up."

"That should work," he agreed. His smile faded, and he looked at her with an intensity that made her shiver. "I may be a little hardheaded at times, but understand this, Jo. I'll never try to stand in your way or keep you from going where you need to go, as long as you remember where your home is."

She nodded and brushed tender fingers against his cheek, her heart overflowing with love. "My home is with you, Rob, now and forever."

His arms closed around her, and she felt his shoulders shake with emotion, felt his love settle around her like a warm cloak. "That's good," he whispered, "because that's how long it will take to show you how much I love you."